CRIME AND THE LAW

A Look at the Criminal Justice System
by Maxine Phillips

The Peoples Publishing Group, Inc.

Free to Learn, to Grow, to Change

The Realities of Criminal Law (and How to Avoid Them) on a Teenage Reading Level

**Each of the Four Parts of this
New Edition of *Crime & the Law*
Opens with Learning Objectives,
a Cooperative Learning Activity,
and a Role-Play
to Draw Students In on a Personal Level**

ALL 18 CHAPTERS ARE LOADED WITH STUDY AIDS & REAL-LIFE STATISTICS

**A *Case Study*
adapted from a real incident,
kicks off each chapter
to stimulate discussion
& thought.**

Key vocabulary words are easy to learn because
they are highlighted in bold, and may be found in
the glossary in both English and Spanish.

Real Quotes & Advice
from real offenders, victims, & law
enforcement officials bring the voice
of reality into the classroom.

Chapter 5

Being Behind Bars

At age fifty-five, Woody D. was released from prison where he had been for twenty-five years. He had taken the life of a railroad clerk. Before that sentence, Woody had already spent five years behind bars for burglary. He said he had heard people say they wanted to kill themselves while in prison, but he knew he could never do that. He found that if you woke up again every morning, still alive, then you could get through it. Woody made three rules to survive being behind bars: (1) to be strong, (2) to stay calm to avoid going crazy, and (3) to keep out of trouble to be set free on time.

CHECK vocabulary words in blue. LOOK UP word meanings in the glossary beginning on page 92.

CRITICAL THINKING
How can life in prison be even more dangerous than life outside of prison?

Today, Woody is getting to know his three grandchildren. He never had much chance to know his own children while they were growing up. He is now on parole from a life sentence. This means that if he ever commits another crime, he will surely go back to prison for the rest of his life.

In this chapter, you will learn about the U.S. **correctional** system. It is called a correctional system because it is supposed to punish criminals. As a result, the system hopes to improve or correct the way convicts will behave in the future. This system includes more than jails and prisons. Read on to discover what else the correctional system is about and how it is always trying to improve.

The History of Corrections

More than two hundred years ago, there were no jails or prisons in the United States. Punishment for crimes might be public whipping and some other punishment that caused great injury or death to the suspect. Criminals could even be beaten with clubs in front of the whole town or have an ear cut off. They also could have a hot iron burn the letter *T*, for thief, into their skin. Finally, they could even be hanged.

In 1787, the first prison was built in Philadelphia, Pennsylvania. People who broke the law were sent there to work very hard and for no pay. The people in charge of the system thought that the work should be so hard that no one would ever want to commit a crime again. They also thought that making prisoners work hard was better than beating them because hard work would change their **behavior**.

Former offender Woody D. says: "Sometimes I would cry at night, thinking about how I had hurt my family and the family of the man whose life I had taken. Don't get into trouble. It is not worth the pain. You will end up feeling sorry and sad about what you have done."

The People's Publishing Group, Inc.: *Crime and the Law*

ii

This New Edition *of Crime & the Law* is a 4-Part Overview

Plus 2 Activity Book Pages for Every Chapter!

Self-Check — **The first page is a thorough pencil-&-paper review of the chapter. (Use it as a chapter test if you wish.)**

Reality Check — **The second page has activities for individuals, writing, and peers or small groups.**

Many people want criminals locked up for longer and longer sentences. As a result, prisons are more crowded than ever. This is one of the reasons the people who run the prisons want to get people out sooner, not later. But they need to feel that the prisoners who do get out will not be violent.

There are programs for nonviolent prisoners who have almost finished their sentences. Sometimes, such people are sent to halfway houses. Halfway houses are half like a prison and half like a home and usually found in a city, unlike prisons. But they also have rules, and the prisoners have to stay there at night. Prisoners can spend time learning and practicing what to do in the outside world. For example, prisoners might go to hunt for a job or take classes in school.

Sometimes, prisoners are allowed to work at a job and return to prison at night. Some prisons allow prisoners to go home on weekends. These programs try to help prisoners get ready for the time when they return to society.

Often, prisoners are let out of prison on **parole**. This means that they get out before their sentence is over. They have to report to a parole officer every week. If they commit a crime or break the rules of parole, they can be sent right back to prison. For example, if a person misses even one visit, he can be sent back.

After Leaving Prison

It can be hard to go back to your old neighborhood after being in prison. If you were convicted of a felony, you will have a hard time finding a job. Many places do not want to hire people who have been in prison even for a short time.

When you see your old friends again, you may find that they still want you to do the same illegal things that sent you to prison. Watch out! People like this are not your friends!

You might have a hard time getting to know your family again. Your children will have grown up. They may not know you anymore.

If you have a relative who is coming home from prison, you may not be sure how to talk to that person. You may feel embarrassed. You can think about ways to help the person keep from being sad or discouraged. Help the person stay busy and make new friends.

It is very hard to survive and feel comfortable in prison. But it is sometimes even harder to stay out of prison. Sadly, almost half the people who get out of prison end up back there.

Understanding Chapter 5

1. Why are there prisons?
2. What are the different types of prisons?
3. How can programs help a person prepare to go back to life in society?

CRITICAL THINKING
The Uniform Crime Reporting Program of the FBI tells us that some 35 percent of prisoners were under the influence of a serious illegal drug at the time of the crime. Which of these statements is true: Drugs cause crime, or people commit crimes in order to get drugs?

DID YOU KNOW? Three out of every four adult criminals committed their first crime when they were young.

Workbook
Self-Check p. 12
Reality Check p. 13

EYE OPENER The overall ratio of men to women behind bars is about 18:1.

Critical Thinking **occurs at least twice in each Chapter, stimulating thought & discussion about the consequences of one's actions.**

Did You Know **gives factual background, laws, cases, & fascinating information that puts the law into perspective.**

End-of-Chapter Questions
3 review questions per chapter are a check on comprehension.

Eye Opener
Statistics that will shock anyone into action.

Credits:

Editing and feature research by Jocelyn Chu
Copyediting by Salvatore Allocco
Editorial assistance by Daniel Ortiz, Jr.
Production by Doreen E. Smith
Academic consulting by Dr. Charles Lindner and Dr. Jerome Storch
Case study graphics by Peter Cheung
Design by Doreen E. Smith and Jocelyn Chu
Photo Research by Daniel Ortiz, Jr. and Jocelyn Chu
Spanish translation by Nora Adams, court interpreter and translator
Cover Design by Susan Marshall and Klaus Spitzenberger/Westchester Graphic Group
Electronic Publishing Consulting by Doreen E. Smith, James Fee Langendoen, Tony S. Chu, and Art Currim
Logo Design by Wendy E. Kury

Acknowledgments:

A special thanks to the following individuals for their generous contribution of time, effort, and assistance in photo acquisition: Mr. Roberto Roman, Public Relations Specialist, Department of Public Relations, the New York City; Department of Correction, New York City, the New York City Transit Police, Brooklyn, New York; Peter Dodenhoff, Editor, Law Enforcement News, New York, New York; and the Drug Enforcement Administration (DEA), Washington, DC.

Photo Credits:

pg. 2,10,11,43,48,58,65,84,89, N.Y. City Transit Police, Clarence L. Hayes and Maureen McMahon; pg.4,U.S. Dept. of Justice; pg. 7, F.S.A of America; pg.12, Houston,TX Police Dept.; pg.12, Sacramento, CA Police Dept.; pg.12, Detroit, MI Police Dept.; pg. 15, Caris Lester; pg.15,39,76,Richard Farnsworth; pg.16,Courtesy Washington Convention and Visitors Association; pg.17,22,National Geographic Society,Courtesy of The Supreme Court Historical Society; pg. 17,41,42,66,71,78,86,87,PPG File Photo; pg.17, Courtesy of N.Y. State Supreme Court; pg.18, James L. Shaffer; pg.20,27,82,Courtesy of the Drug Enforcement Administration; pg.24, Dick Steffans; pg.26,46,54,N.Y. City Dept. of Correction; pg.31,66, Robert Maust; pg.35,70,John Maher/The Stock Market; pg.40, Laura Sikes/Sygma; pg.49,Paul Conklin/Photo Edit; pg.52, 1980 Betty Medsger;pg.52, Ernie Danek; pg.62,82, Vanucci Foto Service; pg.67, Taylor Archives; pg. 90, Jocelyn Chu; pg. 75, Dept. of Health and Human Services; pg. 72, Paul Schrock.

ISBN   156256-205-3

Copyright 1995

The People's Publishing Group, Inc.
299 Market Street
Saddle Brook, New Jersey 07663-5312

Printed in the United States of America

20 19 18 17

TABLE OF CONTENTS

IN THIS PART, YOU WILL LEARN

■What your legal rights are   ■How search and seizure works   ■What happens when a person is arrested   ■What lawyers can and cannot do   ■What happens in a court trial and with sentencing   ■How you can stop crime

The Criminal Justice System

COOPERATIVE LEARNING ACTIVITY

Is this a recipe for disaster?

EMPOWER YOURSELF Can you imagine what it would be like to choose the end or outcome of a TV movie using the remote control? Where you actually had the power to decide what finally happened? Explore with your small group the scene below from just such a movie and find out.

The Scene: You, Tom, are at your locker in school. You see something in the open locker of another student, Jeff, that you really want but could never afford to buy: a designer leather book bag that costs at least $150.00. Just then, Jeff passes by, harassing you with nasty words about the color of your skin. For moment, you think: "This person has been bothering me for weeks. I owe him one!" You know you keep a small pocket knife in your locker. But rumor has it that Jeff has a gun.

Is this a recipe for disaster? You decide the outcome:

1. Take a vote to see whether or not your group thinks this scene is headed for disaster.

2. Next, stop the action where Tom first sees the book bag. Help him consider or weigh all of the possible outcomes, both good and bad by writing a list of at least three. Start each possible outcome with the words, "what if."

3. Next, in your group, vote on the outcome you think is the best. For example, one "what if" might be Tom deciding a book bag is not worth risking his life. A reasons to chose this as the best outcome might be that it shows *maturity*.

4. Practice a role-play of your group's best outcome. Present it to the others. Be prepared to defend or explain your choice.

While reading this chapter...
Stop and think about attitudes and actions that really gives you power.

Chapter 1

What Is Crime?

A man and woman robbed a grocery store with guns. As they left the store, they ran into a father and his three-year-old daughter. The father happened to be a police officer. One robber ran away. The police officer pulled out his gun. The other robber, Ann B., shot at the officer. Instead, the child was killed by the bullet.

What **crimes**, if any, were committed in this case? Was the robber who ran away **guilty** of murder? What do you think?

CHECK vocabulary words in bold. LOOK UP word meanings in the glossary beginning on page 92.

CRITICAL THINKING

Go back fifty years to when your grandparents were in school. Which of the following problems do you think their teachers complained the most about: Talking, chewing gum, making noise and running in the halls, poor attendance, or wearing clothing not proper for school? Now, come back to the 1990s. What do you think are the most serious problems teachers have to deal with: Drug abuse, pregnancy and abortion, rape, diseases spread through sex, vandalism, burglary, assault, arson, murder, suicide, drug buying and selling, and gang violence? How have times changed?

Officer Kelly says: "I think TV should clean up its act. So many crime shows focus on unnecessary violence. They don't give any explanation for it, nor do they offer any solutions or remedies to the problems so people can at least learn from the programs. TV sells crime like the advertisers sell soap. I think TV is guilty of the crime of creating a crime climate."

What **crimes** were committed in this case? Was the robber who ran away **guilty** of murder? What do you think? In this chapter, you will learn what a crime is. You will learn about different types of crime and you will learn about the crimes that happen most often.

What Is a Crime?

A crime is an act or action that the law says you may not do. There are both **federal** laws and state laws about crime. If a federal law says a certain act is a crime, then it is a crime in every state. Yet, each state has its own laws about crime and each state decides how to punish each crime.

Society is everything about the way people live in groups—in communities, cities, states, and countries. There are laws against crime because crime hurts society. People make laws to help them live, work, and play together safely and in peace. People elect governments to protect the laws of society. That is why the government **prosecutes** to punish a person found guilty of committing a crime.

Kinds of Crime

Misdemeanors are crimes that are not as serious as **felonies**. Punishment for a misdemeanor is usually less than a year in jail. Punishment for a felony can be many years in prison, or the court may order the **death penalty**.

Even less serious than a misdemeanor is a **violation,** or infraction. If a person throws trash on the sidewalk or honks a car horn near a hospital, that person can be punished for a violation or infraction, but the person will not get a **criminal record**.

Having a record means that when a person looks for a job, he has to tell employers he has been convicted. People **convicted** of a felony or misdemeanor will have a criminal record. People with a criminal record may not be allowed to work at certain jobs.

There are many traffic violations or infractions that people should know about. A person may receive a ticket or a **summons** that tells when to appear in court. The court will decide the punishment.

Crimes of Omission: Can you commit a crime by not doing something? The answer is yes. For example, if you do not file your income taxes, it is a crime. It is a crime if you do not stop the car when in an automobile accident. These are called crimes of omission. Omission means to leave something out or not do something you should have. It means not taking the responsibility that should be taken in a situation.

Finally, it is illegal even to try to commit a crime. For example, if a person tries to shoot someone but misses, the person is not guilty of murder. Yet, he is still guilty of attempted murder, or trying to commit a murder. This means that the intent of the shooter is as important as the result of the shooting.

Crimes Against People

The most serious crime against a person is the taking of that person's life. This is called **homicide**. There are three kinds of homicide— murder, **manslaughter**, and negligent homicide.

What is murder? Murder means that the murderer had feelings toward the victim that were bad enough to result in a planned killing.

What is manslaughter? Manslaughter happens when one person does not wish another harm, yet causes the other person to lose his life. There are two types of manslaughter: in involuntary manslaughter, the murderer clearly killed, but without a plan; in voluntary manslaughter, a life is taken because someone behaves in a dangerous way and someone is killed. For example, playing with a loaded gun can result in involuntary manslaughter, even though the death is an accident.

What is negligent homicide? Negligent homicide happens when people are so careless that they cause death. For example, driving dangerously and killing someone because of your driving can be negligent homicide. **Negligence** means not being careful or responsible.

Look back at the story at the beginning of this chapter. It involved two robbers and the murder of a three-year-old who was with her father, a police officer (see page 9). Both robbers were tried in court and convicted of murder. They had not planned to kill the little girl. They had no idea she would have even been on the scene. One of the robbers was not even near her.

Yet, the law says that if a person kills someone while committing a felony, the person can still be **charged** with murder.

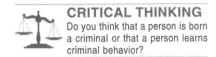

CRITICAL THINKING
Do you think that a person is born a criminal or that a person learns criminal behavior?

DID YOU KNOW? Three out of every four adult criminals committed their first crime before age fifteen.

EYE OPENER Some 45 percent of homicides reported during the 1980s involved handguns. Homicide is the leading cause of death for young African American men in this country.

Also, all of the people involved in the felony can be charged with murder.

Is taking a life always a crime? The answer is no. Self-defense is not a crime. If a person is shown to have killed only because he believed his life was in danger, it can be called self-defense. However, self-defense must be proved in court, and this can be very difficult to do.

What are some other crimes against the person besides homicide? There are several kinds: **assault**, **battery,** and **rape**. All three are very serious.

Assault is an attempt or a threat to attack another person physically. Battery is unlawful or illegal physical contact by one person with another when the other person does not agree to it. For example, if one person threatens to beat up another, she has committed the crime of assault. If she also actually hits him, then she has also committed the crime of battery. You need to check the laws in your state for the exact definition of both assault and battery.

Rape is a very violent crime against another person. It happens when a person forces another person to have sex. Statutory rape happens when a person has sex with another person who is below the age of consent, or too young by law, to have sex. Many states have changed their rape laws to be called sexual assault laws. Rape is violent both in a physical and in an emotional way.

There are laws in some states that give great punishment for crimes committed against a person because of that person's race, religion, or sex. These are called **bias crimes**. Bias means to be against someone for no good reason. Other words for bias are prejudice and hate. For example, recently, a group of white youths attacked an African American child and painted her face with white paint. They were found guilty of assault. But they had also committed a bias or hate crime.

Crimes Against Property

What about crimes that harm things people own? You have already learned about crimes that harm people physically. Crimes against property happen when property is destroyed or stolen. For example, burning another person's property on purpose is called **arson**. Most states have laws against burning your own property, too! Doing damage or harm to someone's property on purpose, such as breaking windows, is an example of **vandalism.** Vandalism can be either a misdemeanor or a felony.

There are other crimes against property, too. For example, breaking into any building in order to commit a crime is called **burglary.**

Stealing or taking anything that does not belong to you is called **larceny**. Petty larceny is stealing something small, usually something worth less than $100. Grand larceny is stealing something of greater value.

White-Collar Crime: White-collar crimes are called this because they are connected with business offices or political areas where many

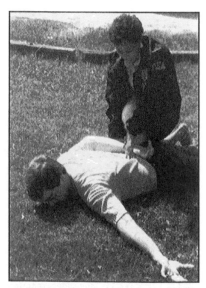

The United States is the most violent nation in the Western world. Every two years, people with guns kill more Americans than died during the entire Vietnam War.

people supposedly wear shirts or blouses with white collars. White-collar criminals steal more than $100 billion a year!

What are some kinds of white-collar crimes? Embezzlement is one. Embezzlement is taking property that you have been trusted to take care of. For example, if you work in a bank and take money from the cash drawer, you are guilty of this crime. If you write a check and sign someone else's name on it without permission, then you have committed the crime of **forgery.** Forgery means changing a writing or document in order to cheat someone of property.

A new kind of white-collar crime involves computers. A person can "break into" computer files just as a burglar breaks into a house. This is how people steal or get information that is private and does not belong to them. Information in computer files is like property.

Extortion is the threatening of others in order to get their property. For instance, the criminal might say, "I'll break your arm unless you give me drugs."

Did you know that receiving stolen property is also a crime? To buy something that you think may be stolen, either in a store or on the street, is a crime. Remember what a felony is and what a misdemeanor is. To receive stolen property is a felony if the stolen property is worth more than $100. It is a misdemeanor if the stolen property is worth less than $100.

What are crimes against public order and safety? Public order is what keeps streets safe, orderly, and peaceful. Most of the crimes against public order and safety are misdemeanors. Yet, there are almost a million arrests for these offenses every year! Disturbing the peace by making lots of noise or being drunk, helpless, or loitering (hanging out on a street or any public place) in a way that bothers other people can also be called a crime against public order.

Crimes Against Society: Laws are made to protect all the people in society. However, not everyone agrees on which laws best protect the most people. For example, some people think that taking drugs does not hurt society. Yet, it is a crime to have certain drugs, to distribute them, or to sell them. Some people believe that there is more crime because drug users commit crimes in order to get money to buy drugs. Others think that the drugs themselves drive people to commit crimes. What do you think? Can both of these be true?

Juvenile Justice

Juvenile delinquency is an act committed by a juvenile that would be a crime if committed by an adult. A status offense is an act that is considered an offense when done by a juvenile, but not when done by an adult. Infractions or violations are not crimes. Yet, when done by an adult, they can sometimes result in that person being put behind bars.

There are special courts for juveniles called juvenile courts or family courts. The reason these courts were set up is that some people believed juveniles needed to be treated differently from adults. They thought

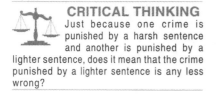

CRITICAL THINKING
Just because one crime is punished by a harsh sentence and another is punished by a lighter sentence, does it mean that the crime punished by a lighter sentence is any less wrong?

that juveniles could still change their behavior if they were helped instead of just punished.

Today, many people are worried about the increase in violent crime committed by youths or juveniles. They believe the juvenile courts have to change. They believe the courts need to punish guilty juveniles more often than before in order to protect society.

Finally, anyone who attempts or tries to commit a crime is guilty. It is illegal to try to shoot someone even if you miss. This means that the intent or plan of the shooter is as important as the result of the shooting.

 Workbook

Self-Check p. 4
Reality-Check p.5

Understanding Chapter 1
1. What is a crime?
2. What is the difference between a state law and a federal law?
3. What are the legal names for serious and less serious crimes?

Chapter 2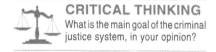
Who Is Responsible for a Crime?

Ten-year-old Omar S. was watching a TV movie with a friend. The people in the movie were playing a game with guns that were not real. Omar's friend said, "We can do that!" He went home to get a real gun to show Omar. The gun did not belong to him. It belonged to his father. Omar's friend tried to unlock the gun. It went off by accident, shooting Omar and killing him.

Did Omar's friend commit murder? Was it just an accident? In this chapter, you will discover just how the law decides whether a crime has been committed in situations like this. It will tell who is **responsible** for committing the crime.

How does the law decide whether a crime has been committed? In most cases, a crime has been committed if (1) an **unlawful** act was committed and (2) the person planned to commit the unlawful act.

For a person to be responsible for a crime, the law says the person had to know what she was doing at the time.

However, you do not have to know that the act is unlawful to be guilty. For example, suppose you are driving 65 miles per hour, which is legal in the state where you live, in a state where the speed limit is only 55 miles per hour. If the police stop you, can you say that you did not know the speed limit? The answer is no.

The law says that people show know the laws. It is everyone's responsibility to learn about them. When something is a responsibility, there is no good excuse for not knowing the right thing to do or not do.

Who is not responsible for a crime? The law says a person must have **intent** to commit a crime. Intent means that a person knows what he or she is doing. Here are some groups of people who usually do not have intent or a reason to commit a crime.

Children. Very young children are not usually held responsible for crimes. Children who commit crimes are usually sent to juvenile court. Each state says how old a child can be and still go to juvenile court. The

CHECK vocabulary words in bold. LOOK UP word meanings in the glossary beginning on page 92.

CRITICAL THINKING
What is the main goal of the criminal justice system, in your opinion?

Former offender Teddy E. says: "I was in prison for murder. Now I help teens deal with the police in a positive way. I see a connection between communities and prison. Poor neighborhoods, broken homes and over-crowded schools all put fuel into the anger of young people."

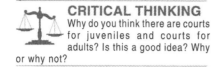
age can be under eighteen, under seventeen, or under sixteen. Make sure to check the law in your state.

People who are mentally ill or mentally slow. It may be decided that a person is not able to know the difference between right and wrong. That person is **judged** not able to have the intent to commit a crime.

People who make a mistake of fact. Suppose that you had some money you did not know was fake, or **counterfeit**, money. If you then bought something with this money, would that be a crime? The answer is no. However, if you *knew* you were spending counterfeit money, then you would be guilty.

People who are forced into an action. Suppose that a bank robber jumped into your car. Chances are you would be surprised and afraid. If the robber then threatened to shoot you if you did not help him get away, would you be guilty of helping this person to escape because you did not stop the car? The answer is no. You would have been forced to act and would not have had a choice. It never was your intent to commit a crime.

People who act in self-defense. Did you know that you are allowed to use some physical force to defend or protect yourself or your property? However, the exact amount of force that may be used depends on the situation. Every situation is different. You may be found guilty of a crime if you use more force than the law allows for that situation. Always use your judgment.

Did Omar's friend commit a crime? Remember the story of Omar and his friend who were watching TV? The law said that Omar's friend did not commit a crime. The friend was young, and, more important, the killing was an accident. However, Omar's parents were very upset. They did not think the law was fair. They wanted the friend's parents to be responsible for the accident.

What did Omar's parents do to make things better for society? They worked to change the law so that parents would be responsible for having loaded guns in the house. At first, they did not succeed. It was not easy. Soon after their son's death, three more children were killed in gun accidents. Finally, the state passed a law making parents responsible for gun injuries caused by their children. This seemed to be more fair for everyone.

Too Young for Adult Court

What if you are too young to be tried in adult court? You have already learned that when someone who is too young to go to adult court commits a crime, that person goes to juvenile court. In juvenile court, youths do not have the exact same rights that adults have in adult court. (See Chapter 4 on the courts.) Also, juvenile court records are kept private, or **confidential**. This means that you do not ever have to tell anyone if you have been convicted in juvenile court. Usually, no one can find out this information.

If you are convicted in juvenile court, you will be sent to a training school. A training school is supposed to be more like a school than a jail. You could be **sentenced** to stay there until the age of twenty-one. For example, Gerald G. was a fifteen-year-old who made nasty, obscene phone calls to a neighbor. The neighbor became very angry and asked the police to arrest him. Gerald was taken to juvenile court and was sentenced to six years in a training school.

If an adult had committed the same crime as Gerald, the adult might not have gone to jail. Gerald fought the juvenile court decision. His case went up to a higher court called the **U.S. Supreme Court**. The Supreme Court said that a juvenile could not be given a longer sentence than an adult for the same offense.

Can juveniles be sent to adult court? This may seem like a puzzle more than a question. However, the answer is yes. More and more juveniles are being sent to adult court. There have even been cases of twelve- and thirteen-year-olds being sent to adult court for committing crimes such as murder and rape. Juvenile justice and adult justice try to be equally fair. Some of the rules and results for criminals are different.

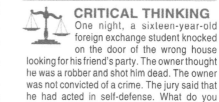

CRITICAL THINKING One night, a sixteen-year-old foreign exchange student knocked on the door of the wrong house looking for his friend's party. The owner thought he was a robber and shot him dead. The owner was not convicted of a crime. The jury said that he had acted in self-defense. What do you think?

DID YOU KNOW? Many violent crimes are committed by people who are acquainted with their victims.

Understanding Chapter 2

1. How does the law decide a crime has been committed?
2. Who not held responsible for committing a crime, and why?
3. Can juveniles be sent to adult court? Explain.

 Workbook
Self-Check p. 6
Reality-Check p.7

Chapter 3

The Police and You

Officer Lee was riding in a police car with his partner, Officer Ho. Suddenly, a voice came over the car radio. There had been a robbery at Main and 8th streets. Two people with guns had held up a grocery store. When Officer Lee turned the car down Main Street, the officers saw them running down the street. One of them ran to a nearby pier and jumped onto a motorboat. Officer Ho leaped out of the car to pursue her. Officer Lee radioed the information to the police station.

CHECK vocabulary words in bold. LOOK UP word meanings in the glossary, beginning on page 92.

What would happen next? This is how many television shows and movies start. You see the police riding around in a car. Then suddenly, there is danger, lots of danger. The music becomes louder. It seems so very exciting.

But is what you see on the screen what police work is really like? The answer is no. Police work is very different from what you see on your favorite shows. In this chapter, you will learn about what a police, or law-enforcement, officer really does at work. You will also explore the problems police have to solve every day.

The police are the first part of the criminal justice system that most people see and know about. The other parts of the system are the courts and something called corrections. (See Chapters 4 and 5 on courts, jails, and prisons.)

The Story of Police Work

How long have there been police in this country to protect society? Two hundred years ago, there were no police. However, some cities hired men to keep the peace. They were paid by the **fines,** or money they collected from people who had broken laws.

Our system of police comes from England. In 1838, the city of Boston set up its first police force. New York started one in 1845. In the West, there was a lot of crime, but very little law enforcement. Volunteer police tried to stop crimes. Then, as cities grew bigger, sheriffs had to be hired to be in charge of keeping the peace.

CRITICAL THINKING
What would happen if people tried to take the law into their own hands when there was serious trouble in the street?

Officer Ortiz says: "Officers are people too. They may act tough, but they have feelings too. When you are arresting someone, we may have fears about the suspect. Will he talk back or get angry or violent and force an action? My advice to young people is to help keep things cool. Talk things through and avoid trouble."

The People's Publishing Group, Inc.: *Crime and the Law*

Today, there are 250 million people living in United States and almost 40,000 public police agencies. There are also private police agencies that protect private property.

What types of police agencies are there? There are federal, state, and local police agencies. Federal police agencies **enforce,** or make sure people obey federal laws. State police agencies enforce state laws. Local police enforce local laws. The Drug Enforcement Agency works to keep illegal drugs out of this country. The **Immigration** and Naturalization Service (INS) keeps people from coming into the United States illegally. The Federal Bureau of Investigation (FBI) **investigates,** or looks into, crimes for the U.S. Justice Department. These are all examples of federal police agencies. Some other federal police agencies work on federal laws that have to do with (1) alcohol, tobacco, and guns; (2) taxes; (3) mail; and (4) **organized crime**. Organized crime is planned and committed on a large scale, like a business.

State police agencies enforce such state laws as traffic regulations on state highways. They also investigate major crimes, using statewide computers to keep track of criminals.

Here is an example of state police at work: Police officers in New York State recently stopped a man because his truck did not have a license plate. When they questioned the driver, they found a body in the back of the truck. They arrested the man, who confessed to killing many people. The state police started an investigation. Soon, they found bodies of more victims in other parts of the state.

Local police include county and city police. These police do most of the law enforcement around the country. Local police have the job of keeping the peace and of law enforcement in their own area. Counties are larger areas that include several cities.

Other Types of Police

The policeman or policewoman on the corner of your street is a public police officer. Everyone's tax money pays for their work. Private police are hired separately. For example, a person can hire a private detective to find a missing person. Neighborhoods can hire guards to keep streets safe. Banks and stores can hire private police to protect them from robbers. Private police also differ from public police because they do not have the legal power to make arrests or to use physical force. However, like you, they can make citizens arrests.

There are police who do not get paid. Many people who want to do their part to fight crime work as auxiliary police or police helpers. This means that they help the police **patrol** the neighborhoods. They wear uniforms, but they often do not carry a weapon.

The Police Officer

The police officer has two main jobs: (1) to keep the peace and (2) to enforce laws. Most of the time, they patrol certain areas of the city. Keeping the peace while on patrol can mean helping a lost child or

DID YOU KNOW?
1. The Chief of Police in Houston, TX, is Chief Sam Nuchia
2. The Chief of Police in Sacramento, CA, is Chief Arturo Venegas, Jr.
3. The Chief of Police in Detroit, MI, is Chief Isaiah McKinnon

EYE OPENER There are 250 crime laboratories in the country. This is where investig-ators can study evidence from murder, robbery and other serious crime scenes given to them by officers.

breaking up a family fight or chasing a mugger.

The police have to enforce the law. This means they need to stop someone who is driving above the speed limit. They need to issue a summons for throwing garbage on the street. They need to break up groups of people who are standing around or loitering. But there are so many laws that the police can never enforce all of them at all times. Often, they must decide quickly which ones they think are most important at the moment.

Enforcing the laws also means that police must spend much time filling out reports in an office. If someone has been arrested, an officer might have to spend a whole day taking the suspect to court. Much of what police officers do is **routine,** or everyday work. All of it is important to the criminal justice system.

Who Are the Police?

For a long time, most police officers were white and male. Today, police work is being done by men and women of all backgrounds who want to help protect society. Often, a police officer chooses this job to follow in the footsteps of other family members. Police officers are usually persons who have the ability to lead. People who go into police work know that it offers a good living with a bright future.

In doing police work, officers see the worst kinds of human behavior. They see people who commit horrible crimes for no reason. They see a lot of pain and suffering. Officers have to learn to keep strong emotionally. They can do a better job if they do not become too upset about what they see everyday.

Can anyone become a police officer? Police officers have to be in good health and be physically fit. If you wanted to be on the force, this means that you would have to pass some physical tests. There would also be tests of what you know about reading, math, and other important subjects. Police work is not only about physically taking the right action; it is also about thinking carefully in every kind of crime situation.

A lie detector tests your honesty. If you have a felony conviction, you cannot be a police officer. However, if you have committed some illegal acts that are not very serious, you might be able to become a police officer. If you pass all the tests you can then attend a police **academy** to be trained for police work.

What are the dangers of police work? A police officer can work for twenty years and never have to shoot a gun. However, there is always a chance of physical danger. More police are injured when they try to break up family fights than when they try to stop a more serious crime.

How do police handle stress? Another danger of police work is emotional stress. This means being emotionally upset and emotionally tired. Why is there so much stress? The police do a lot of important work for society and often do not receive thanks. Yet, they are expected to be on the constant lookout for danger. They see horrible things most people cannot even imagine. Officers sometimes need to talk to counselors to help them relax or to feel better again. Some officers might decide to spend more time in the office from time to time.

When the police use too much force: When anyone uses too much physical force, it is wrong. When police use too much force in doing their job, it is wrong, too. Because police must always expect danger in a crime situation, they can sometimes make an honest mistake. Police are people, too.

For example, an officer might think a suspect is reaching for a gun when she is reaching for something else. The officer might take the next step too soon and injure the suspect. But police officers are trained to be as fair as they can be without taking the risk of losing their own life.

When the police stop someone who seems to be breaking the law, they can never be certain how dangerous that person could be to his own safety. They can never be certain what he will do next. In minutes or even seconds, they need to decide what necessary physical steps to take. This is not easy to do.

The police need to make sure of two things: (1) that the suspect is treated fairly at all times, yet, (2) that the officers are not in danger of being injured or killed while doing their job. Most of the time, the officers will do the right thing. Sometimes, they are forced to guess, and it turns out that more force is used than was necessary. But this can only be decided or known after those few quick seconds have gone by.

Police in the Future

Most Americans are very afraid of crime. This is so even if they have not been victims of crime. Everyone wants the police to protect him. As long as a person obeys the law, he can be sure that the police are his best friend, in any emergency.

But, there is less money to pay for police these days. As a result, many police departments have fewer police than they had ten years ago; many more are needed. This means police will have to try to work more closely with people in their communities to stop crime. There needs to be much more cooperation in the future.

There will also be more women and people of all backgrounds on the force. People who have more education will go into police work more often. Officers will resemble, more closely, the populations and neighborhoods they serve.

Policing used to be about officers merely reacting to crime and violence after it happened. In the 1970s, police worked more in teams. In the 1980s, the goal was crime prevention. Today and tomorrow, police will continue to expand their teamwork into a growing partnership with communities.

Finally, as a result of computer technology, police from around the country and around the world will be able to work more closely with each other. For example, if police in Pennsylvania arrest someone, they can send a picture of the suspect's fingerprints to a central national computer. The computer record will show whether the person has a police record

The People's Publishing Group, Inc.: *Crime and the Law*

CRITICAL THINKING Some people wonder if female officers can do all that male officers do especially in times of physical danger. But there are many ways in which police officers can help each other. What are some of them?

DID YOU KNOW? Interpol is a law-enforcement organization with members from more than 40 countries. It solves crimes on a worldwide level, such crimes as huge drug operations. Begun in 1946, its main office is located in Paris, France.

EYE OPENER In 1991, there were roughly half a million law-enforcement officers in the country.

13

CRITICAL THINKING
A federal crime bill has been proposed which would increase funding for community policing across the country. What effect do you think this will have on the crime rate?

or not. This sharing of information will help keep society safer by helping to convict criminals more quickly. The more efficiently the police can do their job, the more efficiently the courts can carry out the next steps in the criminal justice system.

 *Workbook*

Self-Check p. 8
Reality-Check p.9

☞ **TO LEARN MORE**

The Peoples Guide to Government: Judicial Branch, p. 32

Understanding Chapter 3

1. What are the three levels of police in the United States?

2. Describe what police officers do.

3. Explain some of the dangers of police work.

Chapter 4

The Courts and You

Horatio P. went to a diner to have lunch. He was wearing a brown leather jacket which he removed when he arrived. Later, when ready to leave, Horatio P. saw a brown leather jacket he thought was his. He made a mistake. In the pocket of the coat was some expensive jewelry. When the owner of the coat looked up and saw Horatio, he ran after him. He grabbed Horatio and called for a police officer to arrest him.

At the trial, the judge told the **jury** not to consider whether or not Horatio P. meant to steal the coat. The judge told the jury to think only about whether he had taken the coat and jewelry. The jury found the suspect guilty.

CHECK vocabulary words in bold. LOOK UP word meanings in the glossary, beginning on page 92.

This chapter will tell you about the court system, from trial courts to appeals courts. It will also tell what you should know about juvenile court and juvenile justice.

Unlike English criminal justice, there is no single unit of U.S. criminal justice that covers the whole country or one set of courts, police, and corrections. Instead, there are 51 separate systems, one for each state and another for the federal government.

 CRITICAL THINKING
How would this country be different if there were no criminal justice system, no protection of rights, and no law and order?

Federal and State Courts

There are federal police agencies and state police agencies. So it follows that there is a federal court system and a state court system. The federal system handles federal crimes such as federal robbery, mail robbery, bringing illegal drugs into the country, destroying federal property, and not paying income taxes.

Federal courts also handle crimes that involve people crossing over state boundaries, or border lines, from one state into another—from California to Oregon or from North Dakota into South Dakota. For example, gun dealers sometimes buy guns in a state that has few gun-control laws and take them to a second state that has much stricter gun-control laws. In the second state, people have a harder time buying a gun. As a result, the dealers are able to sell them easily but illegally in the second state.

Former "street kid," Jose C., says: "I was a street youth. I hung out on the corner with my buddies and got into trouble. But my teachers would not give up on me. They encouraged me to be the first person in my family to go to college. Today, I have a successfully criminal law practice. In my spare time, I speak to school and community group all over the United States. I want to do my part to keep street kids avoid becoming juvenile offenders."

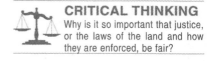

CRITICAL THINKING
Why is it so important that justice, or the laws of the land and how they are enforced, be fair?

State courts deal with crimes committed in that state. A state court cannot try a drug dealer who lives in Kansas for breaking the law in Oklahoma. A federal court must do this.

Trial and Appeals Courts

Both federal and state courts have trial courts and **appellate,** or appeals, courts. The job of the trial courts is to find out the facts or truth in a case. These courts then decide if the accused person is guilty or innocent. If the trial court finds the person guilty, he may be able to **appeal** the **verdict**. This means having the case reviewed or tried a second time by an appeals court.

Steps in the System

The different levels of federal and state courts are like steps in the criminal justice system. Different states may call their courts by different names, but all states have trial courts, appeals courts, juvenile courts, family courts, a probate court, and local courts.

Local courts handle small crimes and civil cases. They may handle the first hearing for a serious criminal case. Local courts also handle traffic offenses. They are also called lower courts because they are the first step in the system.

DID YOU KNOW? For the past two decades, the courts have moved away from rehabilitating or rebuilding lives of offenders towards longer, harsher sentences. Capital punishment has also been used more often.

The highest court in the country is the Supreme Court. If the Supreme Court rules against a suspect, there is no other place to appeal the case. The power of the federal courts is limited by the Constitution to cases based on federal law and to disputes between citizens of different states. Most criminal cases are based on state law. This is why the state courts handle criminal prosecutions.

The president of the United States recommends people to be considered as judges to sit on the Supreme Court. These judges have their jobs for life.

What happens in trial courts and appeals courts? A trial court finds out the facts in a case. Witnesses tell what they saw in giving testimony or **evidence**. Lawyers for each side present arguments. The court decides whether the accused person is guilty or innocent of the charges. The trial may be held in front of, or before, a jury. Sometimes, the trial may be held before a judge only, with no jury present.

The person who fails to win in a trial may appeal her case. But a case can only be appealed if a legal mistake has been made or if the law is found not to agree with the Constitution. An error of law means that someone made a mistake of law during the trial. For example, the judge might have allowed certain evidence to be used that should not have been. Lawyers need to think about these things at the end of every trial.

Remember Horatio P. and the brown leather coat? The judge made a mistake by not telling the jury about that the law that says the accused person has to intend, or mean, to steal the property in order to be guilty. The appeals court reversed the verdict in this case. This means that the appeals court changed the verdict from guilty to not guilty.

EYE OPENER Between 1987 and 1991, juvenile arrests rose by 65 percent.

The People's Publishing Group, Inc.: *Crime and the Law*

16

What can happen in an appeals court? The appeals court can let the ruling of the lower court stay the same. It can also overrule, or change, the lower court ruling from guilty to innocent. Finally, the appeals court can order a brand new trial or can make a brand new ruling or decision.

Sometimes, an appeal is about a constitutional matter or the rights of the accused. For example, if an accused person was illegally searched, the case can then be appealed or taken to the U.S. Supreme Court. This means going from a step in the state criminal justice system to a step in the federal criminal justice system.

Judge Thurgood Marshall was the first African American Supreme Court judge.

The Jury

What is a jury? A jury is a group of people chosen from the community. They are honest, responsible adults who have the job of listening to all the evidence in a case. Then they talk to each other to try to weigh all facts as if trying to balance things on a scale. They ask questions: "Is there more evidence or less evidence on the innocent or the guilty side?" This is how they decide whether the accused person is guilty or not.

Who can serve on a jury? You can be on a jury if you are a citizen of the United States. You must be able to read, write, and understand English. You also must be a registered voter and a county taxpayer. Finally, you must live in the court district where the jury will serve, or do its job. Most states will not let a person serve on a jury who has been convicted of a felony.

There are two kinds of juries: a grand jury and a petit, or small, jury. The grand jury decides whether a case should go to trial. The petit jury is the actual jury at the trial.

Judge Constance Baker Motley is U.S. district judge for the Southern District of New York State.

There are between twelve and twenty-three members on a grand jury. What do they do? They examine, or look at, all the evidence. They decide whether there is enough reason to try a person in court. If there is enough evidence, the grand jury **indicts**, or officially charges, the accused person with a crime. The grand jury is not a trial jury.

The next step is to take the case to trial. However, if the grand jury does not indict the suspect, there is no trial or next step. The case is closed, or over.

Grand juries can also decide whether to arrest someone. They may investigate to see whether a crime was committed. Grand juries meet in secret. Neither the public nor the defendant know what the evidence is. It is the law that people asked to **testify**, or tell what they know, to a grand jury must do so or be punished.

Do grand juries hear all cases? The answer is no. Sometimes, the district attorney decides whether or not there is enough evidence. Then she files something called an information. This is a form officially charging a person with the crime.

What is a petit jury? This is a small jury that has six to twelve people on it. Twelve is the usual number, which is half the size of a grand

Judge Irma V. Santaella is a member of the Supreme Court of New York.

CRITICAL THINKING Why are the following words important: "Do you swear to tell the truth, the whole truth, and nothing but the truth?"

jury. These people listen to all the evidence during the trial. It is their job to decide whether the accused person is guilty or innocent.

Who's Who in Court?

Who are the people you will find in court? Here are the important ones for you to know:

> **defendant**-the person accused of the crime
>
> **defense attorney**-the lawyer for the accused person. This lawyer does not have to prove that the defendant is innocent. She just has to prove that there is **reasonable doubt** or enough reason to believe that he might be innocent in face of the prosecution's evidence.
>
> **district attorney (or prosecuting attorney)** — the lawyer for the state or federal government. This lawyer has to prove beyond a reasonable doubt, or almost 100 percent, that the defendant is guilty.
>
> **judge**-the person who directs everything to do with case from start to finish. The judge is present when the jury is selected. The judge rules, or decides, on questions of law and decides what evidence needs to be explained. She also decides what evidence is OK to use. Finally, she explains the law to the jury so that they can do their job.
>
> **court reporter**-a person who has the job of writing down everything that is said by everyone at the trial. The court reporter sits at a small machine and types out the words very quickly.
>
> **bailiff**-a person who has the job of telling witnesses when to come into the courtroom. The bailiff takes or leads the jury members in and out of the courtroom.
>
> **clerk of the court**-the person who has the job of directing witnesses to swear, or promise, to tell the truth.

DID YOU KNOW? There are at least 90,000 known juveniles with arrest records, according to the Federal Bureau of Investigation (FBI). These youths commit a large number of all violent crimes.

What Happens in a Court Trial?

Before a person goes to trial, there is first a preliminary hearing to decide if a trial is needed. This hearing can be short or long. Sometimes, a preliminary hearing takes only a few minutes.

In a court trial, first, the lawyers for either side makes opening statement to introduce their side. Then, each side has a chance to give evidence, present witnesses, and ask the witnesses questions. The district attorney questions the witnesses, and the defense attorney questions them. This is called a cross-examination.

The Questioning

What really happens during the questioning? The defense attorney tries to make the jury understand where there is reason to doubt what the witnesses have said. For example, if the case is about a robbery, the defense attorney might ask a witness, "Was it dark at the

EYE OPENER The court system is always changing and improving. But look at the following numbers: 2,400 weapons were found in New York City schools alone last year. More ways have to be found to stop crime before it starts. The job of the courts is almost an impossible one.

time of the robbery? If so, how could you possibly have seen the robber clearly?" He gets the jury to think.

Then it is the defense attorney's turn to call the defense witnesses and ask them questions. It is the district attorney's turn to cross-examine. Next, the district attorney finishes for his side of this case by telling the jury all of the reasons why the defendant should be found guilty.

Now, it is the defense attorney's turn to do the same thing for her side of the case. It is her turn to give a closing statement or argument. She tells the jury why there is a reasonable or real doubt that the defendant committed the crime. This means there is a real chance that the accused is innocent. Next, it is the judge's turn to talk to the jury.

What does the judge tell or advise them? He makes sure they know what laws apply to this case. He also describes the possible verdicts that the jury could give. For instance, in a robbery case, the jury might find the person guilty only of breaking and entering, but not of robbery. Sometimes, people will be found guilty of some of the crimes they have been charged with and not guilty for others.

The jury then leaves the courtroom. From this moment on, the members of the jury may not go home or talk to anyone not on the jury until they decide the case. When they decide on a verdict, they all have to agree. If they cannot all agree on a verdict, then they are called a **hung jury**. Then the judge can call the trial a mistrial, which is like a mistake trial. As a result of a mistrial, there might be a new trial. The district attorney might also decide to drop the charges.

If the verdict is guilty, the judge tells when the sentencing for punishment will be.

Do all criminal cases go to trial? Many criminal cases do not go to trial. Chapter 8 will describe what usually happens when you are arrested and go to court. Often, there is **plea bargaining**. The cases that go to trial are very serious crimes. They are also cases where the defendant feels sure that he can prove there is a reasonable or real doubt about his guilt.

Juvenile Court

The first juvenile court in the world met in session in 1899 in Chicago. The idea for a separate, special juvenile court was the work of a group of women who were concerned about the harshness of punishment for children in adult jails.

What happens in juvenile court? If you are a juvenile, your case does not go to a grand jury. There is never a jury in a juvenile court case. First, your case goes to probation officers, social workers, or court officials. Together, they decide whether your case is serious enough for a hearing or whether it can be handled some other way. For instance, if this is your first offense, they may drop the charges against you if you agree to go for counseling or help for your mental health.

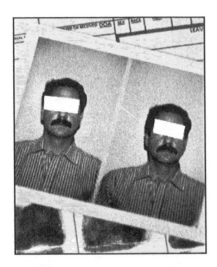

You do not have a right to a lawyer during this first step. However, you do have a right to say nothing. You have the right to talk to your lawyer before you agree to anything. This is very important to remember.

The next step is to have a hearing in front of the judge within the next month or thirty days. The purpose of this hearing is to find all of the facts. You have a right to know what charges are against you. As before, you also have a right to a lawyer. Yet, in juvenile court, you do not have the right to have a jury trial.

You or your lawyer may call witnesses to help your case. You or your lawyer may cross-examine or question the witnesses.

Your rights do not end here. You also have the right to have a copy of everything that is said at the hearing. Most important, you have to be proved guilty beyond a reasonable doubt. You also have the right not to be tried two times for the same offense. (See page 42, Protection against Double Jeopardy.) In most states, you have the right to appeal the verdict.

You do not always have the right to a hearing about whether you should be tried in adult court. Yet, the juvenile court judge may decide that the crime is so serious that you *should* be tried in adult court. Some states have laws that say that certain crimes must be tried in adult court.

After the Hearing

Different things may happen. **(1)** The judge may decide to drop the charges at the first hearing. **(2)** The judge may decide to hold another hearing to tell what he has decided about your case. **(3)** At the second hearing, the court may still drop your case. **(4)** The court may put you on **probation**.

Probation often means being sent to a reform school, a state training school where you learn to change your behavior, or a group home. You have a right to a lawyer at this hearing, too. It is easy to see how your rights as a juvenile follow you through every step of the criminal justice system.

After the hearing is over, the juvenile court record is sealed so that no one can find out about your trial. Then, when you want to find a job, you do not have to tell an employer that you were tried and/or convicted in juvenile court. You have been given another chance to be a lawful citizen and worker who can be respected and trusted in society.

You do not have to commit a crime to go to juvenile court. Parents can go to the court if there is a serious problem in their family. They might need help in getting teens to follow family rules. They might need advice on how to keep things peaceful and nonviolent.

For example, Lee V. had friends whom her mother did not like. She stayed out late with them and argued with her mother about where she went. Her mother was worried that Lee would start to take drugs as her friends did. Lee's mother filed a PINS petition.

PINS means "Person In Need of Supervision." The judge heard all the facts. She thought that Lee's problems could be solved. She told

The People's Publishing Group, Inc.: *Crime and the Law*

Lee's mother about a family counseling program. The counselors helped Lee and her mother work out their difficulties. However, if the court had agreed that Lee was a PINS, she might have been sent to a foster home or a group home.

PINS can be a successful remedy or solution. It is certainly better than having a young person with problems behave out of control and end up behind bars.

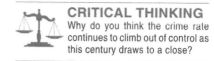

CRITICAL THINKING
Why do you think the crime rate continues to climb out of control as this century draws to a close?

Understanding Chapter 4

1. Describe the different types of courts
2. What is a jury?
3. How is juvenile court different from adult court?

Workbook
Self-Check p10
Reality-Check p.11

  TO LEARN MORE

Government Today, pp. 52-53, 166-113, 140-141
The Peoples Guide to Government: The Judicial Branch, pp. 9-25, 45-51

Turn the page to see how the federal and state court systems are organized.

MEMBERS OF THE SUPREME COURT OF THE UNITED STATES

The members of the Supreme Court of the United States are (left to right): top row: Associate Justices Clarence Thomas, Anthony M. Kennedy, David H. Souter, and Ruth Bader Ginsburg; bottom row: Sandra Day O'Connor, Harry S. Blackmun, William H. Rehnquist, John Paul Stevens and Antonin Scalia Associate Justice Harry S. Blackmun will retire at the end of his current term.

Federal court system

U.S. Supreme Court

Reviews decisions of lower federal courts.
Reviews decisions of highest state courts if
constitutional or federal law issue is involved.

↑

U.S. Courts of Appeals

Review decisions (hear appeals) from U.S.
district courts. There are 13 of these courts.

↑

U.S. District Courts

Try cases involving federal crimes or civil suits.

State court systems

State courts try crimes committed in that state. A state court cannot try someone for breaking the law in another state.

State systems vary. The courts have different names in different states. But there are three or four levels of courts. There are two levels of trial court, and one or two appeals levels.

Here's how state systems look.

U.S. Supreme Court
Hears appeals on constitutional issues.

State Supreme Court or State Court of Appeals
Reviews decisions of lower courts. This can also be called the appellate court.

Intermediate Appellate Court
Reviews decisions of lower court. Not all states have this level.

Trial courts (superior court)
- DISTRICT, COUNTY, OR MUNICIPAL COURT
  hears civil and criminal cases.
- JUVENILE OR FAMILY COURT
  hears domestic and juvenile cases.
- PROBATE COURT
  processes wills and estates.

Local courts
- MAGISTRATES COURT OR JUSTICE OF THE PEACE
  hears minor criminal cases.
- TRAFFIC OR POLICE COURT
  hears minor traffic offenses.
- SMALL CLAIMS
  hears minor civil cases.

Chapter 5

Being Behind Bars

At age fifty-five, Woody D. was released from prison where he had been for twenty-five years. He had killed a railroad clerk. Before that sentence, Woody had already spent five years behind bars for burglary. He said he had heard people say they wanted to kill themselves while in prison, but he knew he could never do that. He found that if you woke up again every morning, still alive, then you could get through it. Woody made three rules to survive behind bars: (1) be strong, (2) stay calm to avoid going crazy, and (3) keep out of trouble to be set free on time.

CHECK vocabulary words in bold. LOOK UP word meanings in the glossary beginning on page 92.

CRITICAL THINKING
How can life in prison be even more dangerous than life outside of prison?

Today, Woody is getting to know his three grandchildren. He never had much chance to know his own children while they were growing up. He is now on parole from a life sentence. This means that if he ever commits another crime, he will surely go back to prison for the rest of his life.

In this chapter, you will learn about the U.S. **correctional** system. It is called a correctional system because it is supposed to punish criminals. As a result, the system hopes to improve or correct the way convicts will behave in the future. This system includes more than jails and prisons. Read on to discover what else the correctional system is about and how it is always trying to improve.

The History of Corrections

More than two hundred years ago, there were no jails or prisons in the United States. Punishment for crimes might be public whipping and some other punishment that caused great injury or death to the suspect. Criminals could even be beaten with clubs in front of the whole town or have an ear cut off. They also could have a hot iron burn the letter *T*, for thief, into their skin. Finally, they could even be hanged.

In 1787, the first prison was built in Philadelphia, Pennsylvania. People who broke the law were sent there to work very hard and for no pay. The people in charge of the system thought that the work should be so hard that no one would ever want to commit a crime again. They also thought that making prisoners work hard was better than beating them because hard work would change their **behavior**.

Former offender Woody D. says: "Sometimes, I would cry at night, thinking about how I had hurt my family and the family of the man whose life I had taken. Don't get into trouble. It is not worth the pain. You will end up feeling sorry and sad about what you have done."

Today, the system still tries to have prisoners work very hard for very little or no pay. It also tries to keep young people separate from older criminals so they cannot learn how to commit more serious crimes from more experienced offenders. There are also different areas and buildings for prisoners. Where they are sent depends on whether they are very dangerous, or not dangerous.

Why are there prisons? Prisons keep criminals away from the rest of society so that they cannot commit more crimes or harm society further. Prison is a strong punishment. Some people believe that prisons should also help people change their ways so that they learn to do something instead of committing crimes. They can learn to help the society they had once harmed.

CRITICAL THINKING
Three out of four women in U.S. prisons are mothers. One out of two of the children of these prisoners never see their mothers while they are behind bars. Explain this statement: "Mothers are not the only ones who are in prison. Their families are too."

Prisons Today

There a difference between prison and jail. People often use these words as if they are the same. But they are different. **Jail** is a place where people are kept for a short time while they wait for a trial or for sentencing. Also, a person who commits a misdemeanor and is sentenced to up to a year can go to jail.

Prisons are for people serving longer sentences. A person who commits a felony goes to prison. There are federal and state prisons just as there are federal and state courts. The federal prisons are for people convicted of federal crimes, and the state prisons are for people convicted of state crimes.

DID YOU KNOW? The fifteen-to-nineteen year age range has the highest rate of criminal offenses. Also, 73 percent are between the ages of eighteen and thirty-four.

There are many kinds of prisons. People who have committed very serious crimes and have long sentences are put into prisons that have thick walls. The prisoners are locked up for the safety of others most of the time. One such prison has a wall that is 30 feet high above the ground and 30 feet below the ground. The wall is also 3 feet thick. No one has ever escaped by going over, under, or through the wall.

Another kind of prison is for people who are judged to be less dangerous. The fences may be made electric so that people trying to climb over them will receive an injury or electric shock.

A third kind of prison is for prisoners who are not dangerous. Here, convicts are more free to move around.

Finally, some prisons for first-time offenders who are not violent are like army camps located in the woods. The prisoners do farm and other outdoor work. The prisoners spend three to six months doing physical exercise and drills and can also get drug treatment. By changing behavior, some people believe that this kind of prison may be able to keep prisoners from committing crimes again when they get out.

Prison drug-treatment programs help. The prisoners help each other to get off and stay off drugs. But there are three rules in this kind of program (1) no violence, (2) no stealing of drugs, and (3) no drug use. If anyone breaks one of the rules, that person must give up all right to the program.

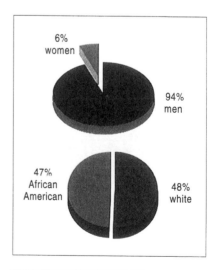

EYE OPENER Of approximately 850,000 criminals in U.S. jails and prisons, about 94 per cent are men, 6 percent are women, 48 percent are white, and 47 percent are African American.

CRITICAL THINKING
Programs like the STEP program (Self-Taught Empowerment and Pride) which includes marching drills, drug counseling and training, have reduced the rate of return to prison. Some 94 percent of those involved in the first year of STEP never returned to prison.

Prison can be a place where you learn job skill, or where you can go to school. Prison can also be a place where you sit in a **cell**, or a small plain room with bars, twenty-three out of twenty-four hours a day only one hour for walking around in the yard outside! However, all prisons are alike in some ways.

In all prisons, nothing you do is private. Everything you do has a rule and all rules must be obeyed. For example, if breakfast is served at five o'clock in the morning, everyone must go to breakfast at exactly that time. Supper may be served at three o'clock in the afternoon. It does not matter whether you are hungry or not at that time. Also, there is no more food to eat until breakfast. Have you ever been hungry? Can you imagine what that would be like?

Prison can be a place that is both dangerous and overcrowded. There really are no rights, no life that is anything like life outside of prison. This means that prisoners have to know how to protect themselves physically. Prisoners have the right to stay safe. Visitors often can only visit by talking through a screen.

DID YOU KNOW? During the last decade, the number of women in prison tripled.

Prisoners might not be allowed to watch television, listen to a radio, or even have anything to read. They might not be allowed to get phone calls from their families. They might also not be able to have more than a few visitors.

Prison can be a place that is very boring. Prison life has the same routine every day, week after week, month after month, year after year. Sometimes, prisoners get so bored they break the rules. If a person breaks the rules, there are special punishment cells. Extra time may also be added to the present sentence. However, if a person follows the rules, the sentence could be made shorter for good behavior.

What is it like to visit someone in prison? If you have a relative or friend in prison, you may want to visit. Usually, there is a long ride to get to the prison. You should learn the rules for a visit before you go so that you will not be upset or afraid when you are there. When you arrive, you will have to be checked by a guard. This may make you feel like a criminal. However, the guards have to do their job. They need to be sure you are not bringing in a knife, a gun, or drugs that could cause more violence and trouble. The best thing to do is to cooperate and obey the rules.

The person you are visiting might be so happy to see you that he or she will show a lot of feelings. You may feel emotional, too. Also, if the person is allowed to get packages, you can bring some gifts — food, soap, or books. But the packages will also be searched.

Preparing to Leave Prison and Go Home: The number of people behind bars in the United States is very high compared with other countries. So many people are shut away and, as a result, cannot help society. No other country has as many people behind bars. This is a national tragedy.

Many people want criminals locked up for longer and longer sentences.

EYE OPENER One out of four prisoners carries the HIV virus. One out of five prisoners carries the TB virus. Although prisoners have the right to stay safe, because of overcrowding and violence behind bars, prisons can be more dangerous than the streets!

The People's Publishing Group, Inc.: *Crime and the Law*

As a result, prisons are more crowded than ever. This is one of the reasons the people who run the prisons want to get people out sooner, not later. But they need to feel that the prisoners who do get out will not be violent.

There are programs for nonviolent prisoners who have almost finished their sentences. Sometimes, such people are sent to halfway houses. Halfway houses are half like a prison and half like a home and usually found in a city, unlike prisons. But they also have rules, and the prisoners have to stay there at night. Prisoners can spend time learning and practicing what to do in the outside world. For example, prisoners might go to hunt for a job or take classes in school.

Sometimes, prisoners are allowed to work at a job and return to prison at night. Some prisons allow prisoners to go home on weekends. These programs try to help prisoners get ready for the time when they return to society.

Often, prisoners are let out of prison on **parole**. This means that they get out before their sentence is over. They have to report to a parole officer every week. If they commit a crime or break the rules of parole, they can be sent right back to prison. For example, if a person misses even one visit, he can be sent back.

CRITICAL THINKING
The Uniform Crime Reporting Program of the FBI tells us that some 35 percent of prisoners were under the influence of a serious illegal drug at the time of the crime. Which of these statements is true: Drugs cause crime, or people commit crimes in order to get drugs?

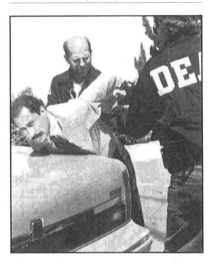

After Leaving Prison

It can be hard to go back to your old neighborhood after being in prison. If you were convicted of a felony, you will have a hard time finding a job. Many places do not want to hire people who have been in prison even for a short time.

When you see your old friends again, you may find that they still want you to do the same illegal things that sent you to prison. Watch out! People like this are not your friends!

You might have a hard time getting to know your family again. Your children will have grown up. They may not know you anymore.

If you have a relative who is coming home from prison, you may not be sure how to talk to that person. You may feel embarrassed. You can think about ways to help the person keep from being sad or discouraged. Help the person stay busy and make new friends.

It is hard to survive in prison. It is sometimes even harder to stay out of prison once you have been released.

DID YOU KNOW? Three out of every four adult criminals committed their first crime when they were young. Also, the overall ratio of men to women behind bars is about 18:1.

Understanding Chapter 5

1. Why are there prisons?
2. What are the different types of prisons?
3. How can programs help a person prepare to go back to life in society?

 Workbook
Self-Check p. 12
Reality-Check p.13

Turn the page to see an overview of the criminal justice system.

Flowchart of the Criminal Justice System

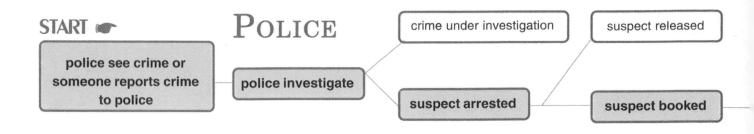

START 👉 **POLICE**

police see crime or someone reports crime to police	→	police investigate

crime under investigation

suspect released

suspect arrested

suspect booked

CORRECTIONS

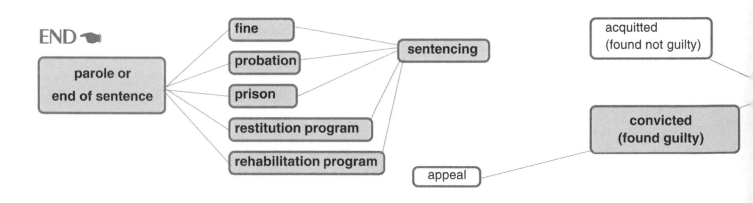

END 👈

parole or end of sentence

- fine
- probation
- prison
- restitution program
- rehabilitation program

sentencing

acquitted (found not guilty)

convicted (found guilty)

appeal

The function of the criminal justice system is to deal with crime and criminals. It also tries to prevent crime from happening. Every year, more juveniles become involved with the system. Because violent crime is the number one public health problem facing our society, all young people should know their rights and responsibilities at every step of the system. It is necessary for all young people to have the necessary skills to deal positively with the police. Almost everyone becomes involved in the criminal justice system as a suspect, a witness, or a victim.

The People's Publishing Group, Inc.: *Crime and the Law*

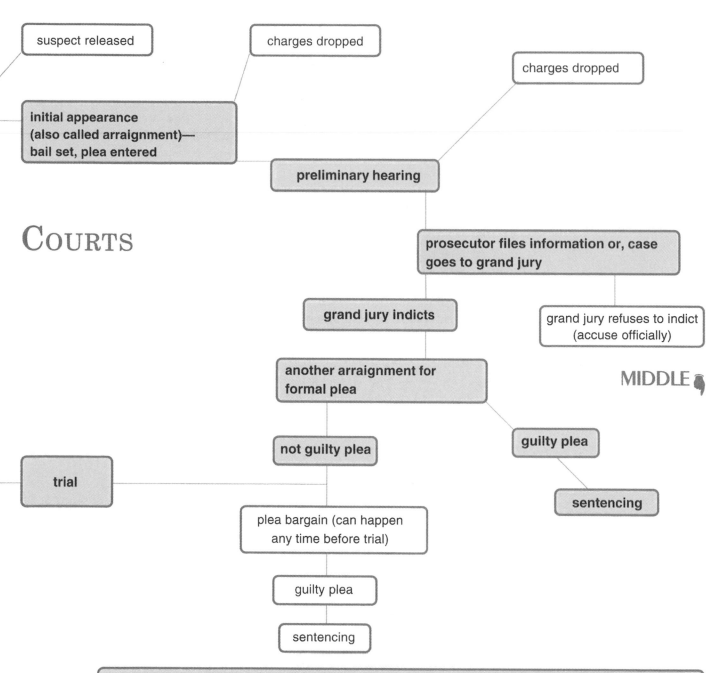

COURTS

The following boxes appear in the flowchart:

- suspect released
- charges dropped
- charges dropped
- initial appearance (also called arraignment)— bail set, plea entered
- preliminary hearing
- prosecutor files information or, case goes to grand jury
- grand jury indicts
- grand jury refuses to indict (accuse officially)
- another arraignment for formal plea
- MIDDLE
- not guilty plea
- guilty plea
- trial
- sentencing
- plea bargain (can happen any time before trial)
- guilty plea
- sentencing

The three parts of the criminal justice system—the police, the courts, and corrections—work together and overlap. For example, even though the police are more involved at the beginning of the process, their role does not end as soon as a case goes to court.

This chart walks you through each step of the system. Just follow the arrow pathway. Any case will follow along some or all of the pathway. A case can be dropped at any point along the pathway.

This chart has many difficult but important words and ideas. Some of them have already been explained in the first part of the book. Review this information carefully and look out for the rest of the words as you work through the book.

IN THIS PART YOU WILL LEARN

■Understand how the police and citizens learn about and form opinions about each other ■Understand how negative images of either the police or the citizens in a community can come about ■Identify ways of improving police-citizen communications in your community ■Know how to tell someone else about how to keep tensions from escalation in police-citizen encounters ■Be able to see yourself as other do in situations that could involve conflict

YOUR RIGHTS IN THE SYSTEM

COOPERATIVE LEARNING ACTIVITY

Gate-keepers to the criminal justice system

EMPOWER YOURSELF

One way in which the police and the public communicate is through the media. The media has a great effect on police-citizen relations. In high crime areas, in the media and in real life, there is much tension between the two. The picture each has of the other can be negative. Explore the scene below with your small group to discover how turning police encounters into a positive experience can mean not having to become involved in the criminal justice system.

Scene: Members of a local street gang watches a TV series every Tuesday night about violent encounters between police and a gang in a small town. The police and the TV gang act like enemies whenever they see each other. There has been a crime wave in the community but no real reason for police to suspect the gang. There is a shootout. Several cops and gang members are killed. There is no solution offered for the violence. The gang members react badly and so do the police. In part, the gang is acting out what it has seen on TV. In this situation, neither police nor gang members used behavior that reduces tension.

Will this program have any effect on the community?
1. In your groups, discuss the kind of negative police-citizen encounter or kinds of meetings on the street that happens most often in your community. Talk about words or actions that build tension.
2. Develop a short role-play of your group's negative encounters. Write a script for it that includes words and actions that cause tension to build or escalate.
3. Role-play your group's encounter for the class. (Videotape it if possible.) Play back the tape at least twice — once to view it — and once to identify words or actions turn that the encounter into a negative one. As a result of analyzing the class role-plays, make a list of opinions or feelings that citizens might have about the police. Write a list of opinions or feelings that police might have about the citizens.
4. Next, choose the subject or issue your group feels causes the most tension or conflict in police-citizen encounters. Develop a TV public-service message that tells people how to improve police-community relations.

While reading this chapter...

Stop and think about the differences between a positive encounter involving talking and a negative encounter that involves confrontation or conflict.

The People's Publishing Group, Inc.: *Crime and the Law*

Chapter 6

How Laws Work

Imagine it is 800 years ago. Imagine you live in a small village in England. A neighbor says you stole some potatoes from her garden. You say that you are not guilty. In order to prove that the accused is telling the truth, it is the custom to have the person stick one hand in a pot of boiling water. If the hand comes out not burned, then people are willing to say the accused is telling the truth. However, if the hand is burned, then the accused will be hanged!

This is what the criminal justice system was like centuries ago. A person could be forced to **confess** to a crime by being tortured. In those days, if you did not have money to pay the fine, you could lose your life! Laws have changed a great deal since then.

In this chapter, you will learn about the history of our laws and of the **Constitution** of the United States. You will discover the different kinds of laws and legal rights everyone has to stay safe and out of prison.

CHECK vocabulary words in bold. LOOK UP word meanings in the glossary beginning on page 92.

The History of Our Laws

Where did our laws come from? Laws in the United States developed or came from English laws. Our legal system is also similar to the Canadian system. This is because the United States and Canada were once colonies of England.

For hundreds of years, laws were not written down or recorded. Most people could neither read nor write. Yet, people always had a strong notion of what was right and what was wrong. Throughout history, people have continued to search for what is fair-for the individual and for society as a whole. Laws regarding fairness in everyday life are called **common laws**.

After the United States broke away from England, it still kept most of English common law. However, the first Congress wrote a constitution for the new country. This new American Constitution became the foundation for our laws. Later, more parts were added to the Constitution. These were called **amendments**.

⚖ **CRITICAL THINKING**
About 61 percent of Americans have not even heard of the Bill of Rights. Why is it important to know about the origins of the laws of this country? How can knowing about the laws of your state and city or town help your life?

Offender Johnson says: "I am behind bars now. Another prisoner in my cell block tried to kill me. But the law says that is attempted murder. Fairness in how laws work means behind bars, too. It is funny: Now that I am here for breaking the law, I realize for the first time why we have laws."

The Bill of Rights

The first ten amendments to the Constitution tell the rights of people in the criminal justice system. They are called the Bill of Rights. The first eight amendments are of the most interest to those learning about the criminal justice system.

The most important right is that of **due process**. This right means that every legal case must follow certain steps that protect every suspect's rights. The right of due process protects against society punishing an innocent person. In the example from 800 years ago, the accused person would not have had a right to due process. Common law of the times would have said that an accused person was guilty unless he could prove he was innocent.

In modern times, an accused person is innocent until proven guilty. This is because, very early on, people decided that this early system of criminal justice was most unfair. They wanted to change the laws. As a result, they made the king of England sign a paper called the *Magna Carta*. This means "Great Charter." Like a constitution, it listed the new rights of the English people. This was the birth of due process.

What does due process mean in the 1990s? It means that everyone has a clear set of rights. These rights include:

1. the right to be told when you are going to court
2. the right to a **hearing**
3. the right to **defend** yourself, or to answer your accuser
4. the right to a jury of people who will be fair
5. the right to a fair trial

Do all other countries have due process? The answer is no. In many societies, everybody must work together to find out who is and who is not guilty. Their legal systems say that the accused person is guilty unless the evidence proves that the person is innocent. In the United States, things are very different.

Two sides present their information on a case in court. These are the prosecution and the defense. They do *not* work together; they work against each other, or compete. This means that each side must argue one side of the thinking as best it can. This is to make sure that nothing important gets left out. As a result, the truth usually gets discovered, and the verdict is fair and just.

The prosecution must prove that a person is guilty beyond any reasonable doubt. On the other hand, the defense in the face of the prosecution's evidence has to prove that there is a reasonable doubt. By having the two sides do this, the criminal justice system feels there is the best chance of finding out who is guilty and who is not.

Another important right that is in the Constitution is the right to **habeas corpus**. *Habeas corpus* is a term that means "you have the body." Today, this right means that a person cannot be put into jail without being charged with a specific crime. The person must be brought in front of a judge in court soon after being arrested. This right makes sure people will not be put into jail for no reason or for not enough of a reason. What is needed in order to keep someone under arrest is called *just cause*.

CRITICAL THINKING
People who support the death penalty argue that it is the best way to punish murderers. They say it frightens other would-be murderers from committing this crime. What is your opinion?

Who Makes Laws?

Our laws are made by the U.S. Congress, which is part of the federal government. They are also created by city and state governments. State legislatures are the units of government that write and pass laws. Laws that are written down are called **statutes**. All of the written laws, together, are called *statutory law*.

How do the Congress and legislatures know what laws to make? The job of the Congress and legislatures is to listen to the people in order to discover and understand the changing needs of society. For example, there are many people whose children or relatives lost their lives because of drunk drivers. These people have made state legislatures change many laws so that drunk drivers must now be given a prison sentence.

Besides statutory law, there is common law and **case law**. Case laws are not written down. Instead, each time a case has been decided, that case becomes part of case law or law that reflects the history of similar cases.

All of our laws must be constitutional. Yet, courts have had some different ideas about just what the Constitution says or means. It is often difficult to decide what parts of the Constitution, if any, need to be reread for new meaning as the decades come and go. Also, society's opinions about many issues and subjects are constantly changing.

DID YOU KNOW? Archaeology, or the exploration of cultural remains, has added much to our knowledge of ancient laws and legal systems. By comparing the criminal justice systems of other times and places in history, modern societies can select the best features of many systems to build the wisest system possible.

The Death Penalty

Is the death penalty constitutional? In the 1970s, the U.S. Supreme Court said that death-penalty laws of most states were not constitutional. It did not say that the death penalty itself was unconstitutional. For ten years, no one was executed in the United States. States changed their laws.

People who were against the death penalty appealed the convictions. This time, the Supreme Court said the laws were constitutional. Now thirty-six states have the death penalty.

Even though the Supreme Court does not yet agree, the judges think that the majority of people still believe that the death penalty is not constitutional. They think this because the Constitution says that any punishment cannot be cruel and unusual and that death is a cruel and unusual punishment to be used in extreme cases only.

This question is one of the most debated legal questions of the decade. It is one that everyone should think about seriously. The right thing to do is not always clear. One thing, though, is clear: society goes back and forth in its thoughts about the death penalty. As other factors change, the economy, family life, the quality of life-opinions change as to whether or not capital punishment is effective in reducing the murder

EYE OPENER Since 1976, the number of prisoners executed for their crimes has been less than thirty-one in a single year. This is according to Todd Clear and George F. Cole in their book, *American Corrections*. Brenner, CA: Wadsworth, 1994.

rate. People will always debate whether or not the taking of human life is ever just or fair. They will always debate whether or not the idea of an "eye for an eye" is a fair one. What do you think?

 Workbook
Self-Check p. 14
Reality-Check p.15

 TO LEARN MORE
Government Today, pp. 46-47
The Peoples Guide to Government: Guide to the Judicial Branch, pp. 29, 38-39

Understanding Chapter 6

1. What is the foundation of all of the laws in the United States?
2. How are statutory law and case law different?
3. Who decides whether or not a law is constitutional?

The People's Publishing Group, Inc.: *Crime and the Law*

Chapter 7

Caution: Not Knowing Your Rights May Be Dangerous to Your Health

In 1961, Clarence G. was arrested and charged with breaking into and entering a pool hall. He had broken in to steal cash from the cigarette machine. In Florida, this is a felony. Not having the money to hire one himself, Clarence G. asked the judge for a lawyer. But the Supreme Court has said that only people accused of more serious crime —for which they could get the death penalty—have the right to a lawyer. Clarence G. had no choice but to defend himself in court. This meant he had to act as his own lawyer. Clarence G. was convicted and sent to prison for five years. However, he wrote to the Supreme Court asking it to review his case. The Supreme Court did so and changed its own ruling in 1963, two years later.

The Supreme Court agreed that the Constitution promises everyone the right to a fair trial, even if they have no money to hire a lawyer on their own. So Clarence G. was set free was given a new trial. This time, Clarence G. had a lawyer and was justly acquitted.

In this chapter, you will learn about the rights that are given to everyone in the Bill of Rights, rights that cannot be taken away. These rights help protect people even when they are accused of crimes. These rights are what make the criminal justice system fair and equal.

CHECK vocabulary words in blue. LOOK UP word meanings in the glossary beginning on page 92.

CRITICAL THINKING
Do you agree that school officials should have the right to set rules and to punish students? How do some of the rules in your school help make your school safer?

Your Rights Under the Law

The Right to Due Process of the Law: The Fifth Amendment of the Constitution gives the accused person the right to due process. This means that you cannot be put in jail or fined without enough reason. This also means you have to go through steps in the law or the legal process. The Fourteenth Amendment to the Constitution says that no state shall take away a person's life, liberty (freedom), or property without due process.

The Right to an Indictment: The Fifth Amendment also says that if you are accused of a felony, you have a right to have a grand jury look at the evidence in your case. The grand jury's job is to indict you, or charge you with the crime, or to drop the case. This means that you cannot be kept in jail if there is no evidence against you to suggest you may be guilty.

Protection Against Double Jeopardy: The Fifth Amendment protects you from double jeopardy. The right against double jeopardy

Attorney Simon says: "There was a time when African Americans were not allowed to serve on a jury. There can be no right to a fair trial if there is no right to a fair jury. Today, the criminal justice system is still questioning what a balanced jury means. You and your lawyer need to be aware of the idea or concept. It can affect the outcome of your trial."

means the right not to be tried a second time for the same crime once you have been **acquitted**, or cleared, of the crime the first time.

The Right to Remain Silent: The Fifth Amendment also gives you the right to say nothing in court that could be used against you. If you do testify and the prosecutor asks a question that could hurt your case or make you seem guilty, you can say that you will not answer it. This can mean that you do not have to testify at your trial.

When you do testify in court, you do so under **oath**. This means that you have promised you will tell the truth, the whole truth, and nothing but the truth. Not telling the truth in court is the crime of **perjury**.

The Right Against Unreasonable Search and Seizure: The Fourth Amendment gives you the right to be searched only if the police have a very good reason to do so. Also, you have the right to be searched only equal in amount to how serious the crime is. If you are suspected of a very serious crime, the police may search you and your property very completely.

Sometimes, lawyers try to show the court how evidence was seized illegally. Any evidence that is searched for or not taken legally cannot be used in court. (See Chapter 8 for more on search and seizure.)

The Right to a Fair Trial: The Sixth Amendment gives an accused person the right to a speedy and public trial. This means that the trial cannot be held in secret. It has to be out in the open to be fair. The trial also must happen as soon as possible, even though the courts usually are very busy.

The Right to a Jury Trial and an Impartial Jury: The Sixth Amendment gives the accused person the right to be judged by a jury that is **impartial**. This means the jury members are not involved in the case and do not have an opinion before the case is heard. For example, if you are accused of robbing someone, a relative of the person who was robbed could not be a member of the jury. Your lawyer can ask not to have a person on the jury if he has a good reason to believe that person could not be fair. Your lawyer may decide that anyone who has even been robbed could not be an impartial juror.

The Constitution says that you have the right to a jury trial in cases that involve more than $20. Yet, the Constitution was written a long time ago. Remember that $20 was a lot of money 200 years ago! Today, a $20 case could be a misdemeanor. Today, you only have the right to a jury trial in cases where you could go to jail as punishment for the crime.

The Right to Counsel: The Sixth Amendment gives an accused person the right to counsel. This means the right to use a lawyer. Another word for a *lawyer* is a *counselor*.

The Right Against Excessive Bail: The Eighth Amendment gives the accused person the right not to have too high a bail. **Bail** is money or property that you give the court in order to stay free after your arrest and until your trial. If you do not show up for the trial, you lose that bail money or property. A suspect does not always have the right to bail because the judge may think that he will appear at the trial.

The People's Publishing Group, Inc.: *Crime and the Law*

The Right Against Cruel and Unusual Punishment: The Eighth Amendment also gives the accused person the right to be protected from too much or too harsh punishment. This means that the punishment has to be equal to the crime. For example, a person who steals $15 should not be sentenced to five years in prison.

Yet, some states now have **mandatory sentencing**. This means that the person will not receive a long or harsh sentence for a first offense. But, if the same individual is convicted of the same crime, he must receive a longer sentence, no matter how small the offense. This is because he is a repeat offender who has not learned a lesson or corrected his behavior.

Your Rights in School

Do you have the same rights in school that you have outside of school? The answer is sometimes. All of your rights outside school remain the same inside school. In addition, school officials may make some of their own rules to keep the school safe and orderly.

For example, a school may have a rule against wearing gold chains or anything expensive that might be stolen. It also has the right to suspend any student who breaks any school rules. This is for the sake of everyone's safety. The school has the right to make such rules. Yet, students still have due process rights.

Here is an example: One day, there was a serious fight in the lunchroom. School property was badly damaged. About seventy-five students were suspended that day. The court said that the students had to be told what the charges against them were and that they would have hearings on those charges. This was due process of law.

Not having a high school diploma can harm your life almost as much as having a felony conviction. It is hard to get a job without one. This is why the Supreme Court often decides that allowing students to continue getting an education is an important thing to consider, along with protecting the rights of all of the students in school.

The seventy-five students were not allowed to attend school for a period of time. They were also sentenced to six months of community service after school.

Do students have the right against unreasonable search and seizure? Students do not have exactly the same search- and-seizure rights in school that they have in their home or elsewhere. If the suspected crime is serious, the school can do a search and seizure.

For example, one state supreme court said that school officials needed to search all student lockers because they were looking for guns in a school filled with violence. Without the search, people might be harmed or even lose their lives. In other words, the search prevented possible violence.

Do students have the right to a lawyer at a school hearing? The Supreme Court has said that if a suspension from class is for more than ten days, then students have the right to a lawyer at a school

CRITICAL THINKING
The right to free speech does not give a person the right to yell "Fire!" with no cause in a theater. Can you explain this?

DID YOU KNOW? Sometimes, there are limits on rights, or at least they are balanced by the right of the courts to guarantee or protect the public good. This can be considered more important. For example, suppose there is a public-health scare related to meat-processing methods. A meat-processing plant's right to protect industrial secrets might be considered less important than the right of the public to know if the plant is clean.

hearing. Some states have this law. Check whether this is a law in your state. However, no court has said that a student has the right to a free lawyer if he or she cannot afford one.

Is a school hearing public or private? Most student hearings are private unless you or your parent or guardian wants it to be public. This is because school records are also private. This means no one can see them unless a parent or guardian agrees. Some courts have said that you can insist on a public hearing. Other courts have said the hearing must be private.

Students have the right to have the punishment be equal to, or fit, the crime. For example, if you are suspended for a long time for something that you think was not a serious offense, you have the right to appeal.

Search and seizure is one of the legal issues that most interest students. The next chapter will tell you still more about what can happen to you in the criminal justice system.

Workbook
Self-Check p. 16
Reality-Check p.17

 TO LEARN MORE
Government Today, pp. 30-31, 109
Our Constitutional Heritage, p. 45

Understanding Chapter 7

1. Name three rights that the Bill of Rights gives everyone.
2. Explain what an impartial jury means.
3. What due process rights do students have in school?

Chapter 8

Search and Seizure

The police were looking for a suspect. The suspect was a man about six feet tall and well built. They had been told he might be hiding at the home of Dollree M. They knocked on her door and she let them in even without a warrant. The police searched everywhere and did not find him. Instead, they found some illegal photos in a drawer in the basement. Dollree M. was arrested. Although **convicted** in court, Dollree appealed, saying that the discovery of the photos had nothing to do with the original reason for the police search —finding a suspect in a separate crime.

The U.S. Supreme Court said that the evidence from the photo album was illegal. This is because the police had no warrant. It decided that the photos were to be kept out of the trial. The court decision in Dollree M.'s case involves the rule that says if the police get evidence illegally, then that evidence cannot be used in court. A rule explains how a law can be used.

In this chapter, you will learn what you must know about your rights when you or your property are searched by the police. You will discover what happens when the police need to search you and your property, or when the police need to take you or your property into custody at school or anywhere else.

CHECK vocabulary words in bold. LOOK UP word meanings in the glossary beginning on page 92.

CRITICAL THINKING
Have you ever heard someone say, "A man's home is his castle"? What does this mean legally? Why do you think that the Constitution protects against unreasonable search and seizure, especially in a person's home?

Search and Seizure

Search means to look for something. The police need to search for evidence to help them solve crimes. They can search people by checking their body, their clothes, or what they are carrying. They sometimes need to search apartments and cars.

Seizure means the taking of a person or property into custody. The person or property becomes evidence to help solve a crime.

For example, if the police are looking for a gun and they find one on a suspect, they might arrest her and take the gun. They may need to seize evidence from her even if they are not yet sure she is the criminal. If you are a victim of a crime — let's say that your purse is stolen and later found in someone's house — then the purse will be evidence. The police will need to seize it until the case is finished.

Officer Ortiz says: "Police have to protect themselves and innocent people. Sometimes, that means asking personal questions. Recently, a couple reported a burglary. I had to search their bedroom, and I could see that they were uncomfortable. I guess they thought I had no respect for their privacy, but I let them know that I had to search it for their safety as well as for my own."

Warrants

However, everything in the criminal justice system tries to be balanced and fair. The Constitution protects people from unreasonable search and seizure. In most cases, the police must have a **search warrant** if they want to search you or your home or your car. A search warrant is a court order giving the police the right to search.

Usually, the warrant says that the police have to search during the day. However, it takes time to get a warrant. Often, the police have to act quickly and do their job without one.

Police do not need a warrant:

■ when making a lawful arrest. If you are arrested for a crime, the police can search you and the area around you for hidden weapons or for evidence.

■ when they stop and **frisk** you. You are stopped and frisked when the police think you may be about to do something illegal. They stop you to make sure that you will not. They frisk, or check, you: this means that they run their hands down your body to look for dangerous weapons. The police do this to prevent criminal behavior from happening.

Probable Cause

For example, a police officer saw two people on a street corner. The people stayed there for a long time. Every ten minutes, one would go into a store and look inside. The police officer thought they might be planning to rob the store, so he stopped and frisked them.

The officer found that both were carrying guns, so he arrested them. The suspects said that the arrest was not legal, but the court said that it was legal. This is because the officer had **probable cause** to think the accused were doing something illegal.

Probable cause means that the officer had a good reason for suspecting what he did. Also, many robberies do start out this way, and police can identify clues and patterns early on. For example:

■ You agree to a search. You might agree to let the police search you, but you cannot agree to let the police search someone else. Also, if you are underage, your parents can agree to a search. However, some states have said that parents cannot agree to a search of your room if you do not agree.

■ The evidence is in plain sight. This means that the evidence must be where the police can see it easily. In Chapter 3, you read the case of the police stopping a driver whose truck did not have a license. There was a dead body in the back of the truck. They did not need a warrant to seize the evidence because it was right there in plain sight.

■ The police are chasing a suspect. However, if the suspect then runs into a building, the police might not be able to tell which apartment the suspect entered. If they do not have to have a warrant to search each apartment or closed space in the building, the police can only look for the suspect in the building hallways.

The People's Publishing Group, Inc.: *Crime and the Law*

■ The police can search a vehicle. A vehicle can be a car, truck, bus, van, or train. However, the police cannot stop any vehicle. They have to have some reason to think that they will find evidence in the vehicles they stop.

■ There is an emergency. An emergency exists when there is danger here and now, for example, when someone calls the police at five minutes to three o'clock and says a bomb will go off in the building at three o'clock The police need to search the building for the bomb right away.

■ If you travel from one country or state to another, you can be searched at the **border**, or edge, of the country or state. This is so the police can stop illegal things from coming into the country or going from state to state. Anyone might be a possible suspect. The bringing of illegal drugs and weapons into this country has become a major challenge to law enforcement agencies.

Airlines are very worried about hijackers. Hijackers are criminals who try to steal airplanes. All airports in the United States search people and luggage for weapons. Always cooperate. Better to be safe than sorry.

What about metal detectors in school? Metal detectors are tools that can search for metal objects such as guns or knives. Schools have the right to use a metal detector to look for weapons to keep schools safe.

You already learned that the law protects you from unreasonable search and seizure. From time to time, the courts add more details or ideas to what this includes. You know about the different rights related to search and seizure at home, at school, in the street, and in your car.

CRITICAL THINKING
In 1949, three police officers came into a man's home without a warrant. They were in a hurry. Someone had told them there were illegal drugs there. The police saw two tablets next to the man's bed and asked what they were. But the man quickly grabbed them and swallowed them. In this way, the suspect destroyed the evidence. The police tried to remove them from his mouth. They rushed him to the hospital to have his stomach pumped. The man was finally convicted for having illegal drugs. The Supreme Court said that the search was legal, but the seizure was unreasonable. Can you explain this verdict?

DID YOU KNOW? The exclusionary rule was developed by the Supreme Court for federal criminal proceedings in 1914. It was extended to all states in 1961. It means that any evidence seized in violation of the Fourth Amendment's prohibition against unreasonable search and seizure cannot be counted.

Being Searched

What should you do if you are searched? Do the right thing. If a police officer should ask to search you, here is what you do.

1. Ask if the police have a warrant. If they do, you must open the door. If they do not, they will need to come in anyway to get information that could help their search. Let them do their job. Cooperate.

2. Do not make trouble for the police. Politely tell them that you do not think they have a right to search you. However, do not ever try to stop the search. You could be charged with resisting arrest. You need to work with the law.

3. When you are asked, give the police your full, correct name and address. You do not need to give any other information. Wait until you have a lawyer with you before you answer any questions. The police know that this is your right.

4. Write down the badge numbers of the police officers. Your lawyer may want to talk to the officers later.

5. Check for witnesses. Tell them your name. Ask them to go to the police station to tell what they witnessed—what they saw or heard or remembered.

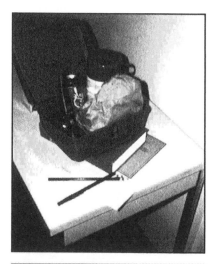

EYE OPENER About 2 percent of students were found to have some kind of weapon in school in a recent nationwide study over a 6-month period.

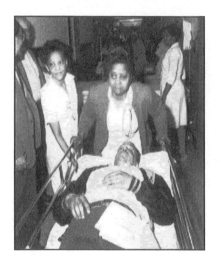

Search and Seizure in School

You have the right against unreasonable search in school. However, if school officials are looking for a weapon, they can frisk you.

Your locker is school property and can legally be searched. Of course, it is never the right thing to bring anything illegal to school. This means drugs and weapons. Drugs have no place in school because drugs ruin the lives of people who sell them or use them. Weapons can kill—even by accident.

Finding Something Illegal

If a person brings something illegal to school and it is discovered, school officials will call her parents or guardian. She does not need to talk about what they have found or answer any questions. However, if the police come, she must give them her name and address. Then, if the police want to arrest her, the school official has to stay with her until a parent or guardian arrives.

Search and seizure is a stressful experience for anyone, but being arrested can be more so. Being behind bars is far worse.

CRITICAL THINKING
Violence is considered a public-health problem, much like smallpox was in the last century. Explain the need for better security in all public places such as airports, libraries, shopping malls, and post offices.

DID YOU KNOW? Statistics on violence and homicide are usually given as nationwide averages. Yet, these statistics may vary from city to city. Crime rates are higher in cities than in rural areas.

Workbook
Self-Check p. 18
Reality-Check p.19

☛ **TO LEARN MORE**
Government Today, pp. 30-31

Understanding Chapter 8

1. What is search and seizure?
2. Explain about a type of evidence that cannot be used in court.
3. What rights do school officials have to search you and your property?

The People's Publishing Group, Inc.: *Crime and the Law*

Chapter 9
What Happens If You Are Arrested

Ernesto Miranda was arrested for kidnapping and rape. The police questioned him for hours. He signed a confession. Later, the confession was used to convict him. Miranda appealed, saying that he had not known his rights. No one had told him he had the right to stay silent. In 1965, the Supreme Court ruled in Miranda's favor.

Now, it is the law that the police must tell an arrested person his or her rights. Because of Ernesto Miranda's case, this is called the *Miranda* rule. The rule says that every suspect who is about to be arrested must be read his or her rights as stated in the *Miranda* warning. How do you know if you are under arrest? What are your rights? What happens after you are arrested? In this chapter, you will learn what happens during an arrest and what a person's due-process rights are. You will learn what happens after an arrest. You will learn correct ways to behave when dealing with the police.

On TV, the police always say, "Don't move. You're under arrest. You have the right to remain silent, and anything you say may be used against you." In real life, the police start by simply questioning you first.

When are you under arrest? You are under **arrest** if and when you cannot leave or are in police **custody**. For example, imagine the police are asking you questions on the street. When you want to leave and they tell you that you cannot go home, this means you are under arrest.

The police will have an **arrest warrant** to take you into custody. The reason for the arrest will be a misdemeanor or a felony they actually saw you commit. They can also arrest you because they have good reason to believe you committed a felony. Finally, the police can arrest a suspect if they have good reason to think a citizen's arrest was lawful. It is proper for law enforcement officers to use their best judgment on the spot.

CHECK vocabulary words in bold. LOOK UP word meanings in the glossary beginning on page 92.

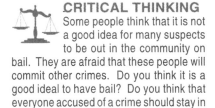

CRITICAL THINKING
Some people think that it is not a good idea for many suspects to be out in the community on bail. They are afraid that these people will commit other crimes. Do you think it is a good ideal to have bail? Do you think that everyone accused of a crime should stay in jail until the trial? Explain.

Officer Goodman says: "Do not argue with the police or make their job hard. Police are just people doing a job. Occas-ionally, they might make a mistake, but no matter what, two wrongs do not make a right. You should always do the right thing!"

Keeping Calm

How do you keep the questioning calm? Many arrests of young people start with a misdemeanor. Sometimes, however, the police might simply see you in a **suspicious** situation that they need explained for safety's sake, for example, the police might see you with a group of friends, late at night, looking in a store window. The police might approach your group and warn you that this is a high drug area. Because of this, they might ask what you are doing there and for your identification. It is their job. They must follow rules about what questions they ask people who might be suspects.

Cooperation

The job of the police is to maintain safety. Your job is to cooperate with them. People who are guilty of something often refuse to respect the police by answering questions or showing identification. This is not a good idea: to do this might make the police think that you have something illegal to hide. As a result, they might frisk you.

If you are innocent and they do not find anything illegal, you still might overreact or become too emotional. This can make the police overreact in turn. Both sides can be afraid and nervous. If things continue to get worse, the police may arrest you for keeping them from doing their job. This does not happen often, but you can make sure that it does not happen to you. Do not stop the police from doing their job. Be polite. Answer all questions. Then leave the area.

Make a choice to do the right thing. Being stopped by the police does not have to be a problem.

Can someone who is not a police officer arrest a private citizen? The answer is yes. Anyone can make a citizen's arrest. For example, a store manager saw a student putting cans of soda into her bag without having paid for them. As she walked toward the door to leave, the manager stopped her to check her book bag. The student refused.

The manager grabbed the bag and found the stolen cans. The student said she wanted to leave, but the manager would not let her. Instead, he called the police. As a private citizen, he did not have to give the *Miranda* warning or follow due process in searching her.

The *Miranda* Warning

What is the *Miranda* Warning? The *Miranda* warning means two things:

1. You have the right to remain silent. You only have to give your name and address. Anything you say may be used against you; that is why you must not say more.

2. You have a right a lawyer. Do not answer any questions until a lawyer is with you. If you cannot afford a lawyer, the state will get one for you. You can tell the police, and they will get one for you.

What if someone you know is arrested? If a friend or relative calls you from the police station because they have just been arrested and need help, remember these three things:

1. Do not ask the person to tell you what happened. Someone might overhear the suspect talking to you. What they say can be used against them. You might even have to testify later about what the person said to you.

2. Call a lawyer. If the suspect cannot afford a lawyer, call Legal Services or Legal Aid in your community. They cost nothing.

3. Go to the police station. If the police question you or the person they arrested, wait until the suspect has a lawyer before you answer. Talking after an arrest can change the case or make things worse.

CRITICAL THINKING
The average prisoner is younger and less well educated than the general public. Why do you think this is so?

The Police Station

What happens at the police station? If you are arrested, the police will take you to the police station. They will fill out papers about the arrest. This is called **booking** you. They will also take your fingerprints and may take your picture.

You will be allowed one or two phone calls. If you have a lawyer, this is the time to call. If you do not have a lawyer, call a friend or family member right away to get one for you. If you cannot afford a lawyer, tell the police.

The police will take your belongings into custody. They will take your clothes, wallet, purse, and whatever else you have. They will give you a receipt that lists everything they found on your person. Your property will be returned to you later.

The police may ask you to be in a **lineup**. They will put you with other people who will be about the same size or appearance as you. They will then ask a witness to pick out from all of the people in the lineup the person who committed the crime. If the police tell you to be in a lineup, ask for a lawyer. The lawyer can make sure the lineup is done in the fairest way possible.

DID YOU KNOW? Crime statistics, like many other kinds of statistics, take much research and survey work. That is why the information for a current year is not available for the general public for at least two years.

Will there be a record of your arrest? The answer is yes. Even if the charges are dropped the next day, this record can harm your life. Many job applications ask whether you have ever been arrested. Your fingerprints will be on file even if you are never convicted.

The police check your fingerprints to see if you already have an arrest or conviction record. An employer can also choose to check your fingerprints, too.

Some states have laws that let you clear the record if you are not convicted. If the arrest was unlawful, the record can be erased or cleared. Find out your state's laws. Of course, the best thing is not to be arrested in the first place.

Going to Court

You have the right to go before a judge as soon as possible. This can be the same day as your arrest, or, if you are arrested on a weekend,

EYE OPENER According to the Statistical Abstract from 1992 of the U.S. District Courts, of the people arrested for burglary, less than 2 percent were acquitted.

CRITICAL THINKING
How can your right to stay silent protect you during the first few minutes after your arrest?

Monday morning. Your first appearance in court is often called an **arraignment.** The reason for an arraignment is:

■ to make sure you are the person charged with the crime. There must be no mistake.

■ to let you hear the charges against you so that you can say whether you are guilty or not guilty. This is called a **plea**. If you have committed a felony, you will make a plea at a second hearing.

■ to set bail. Bail is money or property that you will need to give the court in trust that you will show up for the trial. Bail equals how much you are trusted to keep your word.

■ to give you a lawyer to defend your case.

If you do not have a lawyer yet, do not make a plea without a lawyer! The judge will ask questions about how much money you have. She will decide whether you should have a court-appointed lawyer. The judge will delay the case until you have a lawyer.

DID YOU KNOW? The concept of bail is not a modern one: In the earlier system of criminal justice, there were various forms of release for people awaiting trial.

The judge should also set bail. It is not supposed to be too much money. However, if you are charged with a serious or violent crime, the judge may want to be sure that you will show up for the trial. She might decide to not set bail, and you will have to stay in jail.

Bail

How does bail work? Do you have to give all of the bail money? Most of the time you have to give 10 percent. You have to show that you or your family would be able to pay all of it if you did not come to the trial. For example, if bail is set at $500, you will have to give, or put up, $50. If you show up for the trial and can prove you be trusted, you will get most of it back. If you do not, your family has to pay the $500.

What if you do not have the money? You may have to go to a person called a bail-bonds agent. A *bail-bonds agent* is someone who puts up the bail money for you for a fee. There are bail-bond places near every courthouse.

If your offense is not very serious, your lawyer will try to have the judge release you without paying bail. This means that the judge trusts you enough to let you go. Sometimes, judges will do this if you have a job and a family and have lots of reasons to be responsible.

Once you get out on bail, you can work to find evidence and witnesses. People who are out on bail have a better chance of winning their case. If you have a job, you can keep earning money. If you are in school, you can keep going to school. The judge will look at all these facts later when it is time for sentencing. These facts may help you get a lighter sentence.

EYE OPENER Persons under sentence of death must wait on "death row" in prison for their sentences to be carried out. This is according to the Statistical Abstract from 1992 of the U.S. District Courts. This wait, which has been from one to six years, occurs because the legal process allows cases to be appealed.

What is the next step for you? If you have not committed a felony, there should be a **preliminary hearing**. *Preliminary* refers to something that happens before something else, like "first." This hearing happens before the trial. The police or a court official may ask whether you want to waive, or give up, your right to a preliminary hearing. Do not give up this hearing. It is important in the legal process.

Why is a preliminary hearing important? At this hearing, the judge decides whether the prosecution has enough evidence for a case against you. It is also a chance for your lawyer to find out how strong the district attorney's case is against you. If it is a weak case, the charges may be dropped.

First, there must be enough evidence for a grand jury to indict, or charge, you. There does not have to be enough evidence to convict you, but it has to be clear evidence. The state must make a *prima facie* case. *Prima facie* is Latin for "on the face of it." On the face of it, or just looking at it, the case must appear to be strong.

Second, the judge may lower your bail at this hearing. Third, she will set a trial date. However, at the preliminary hearing, you do not have to give any evidence.

When is there another hearing before the trial? If a lawyer believes some evidence was seized illegally, he will say that the evidence should not be used in court. There will then need to be a hearing so that the judge can decide whether the evidence can be used or not.

There also may be another hearing if the charges are lowered or raised. An arraignment may be called where the charge against you could be raised. For example, you may be accused of a burglary in which someone was shot. If the person dies, the charge will change from a burglary to murder.

The charges may also be lowered. You may change your plea. This is what happens in most criminal cases. This happens because of something called plea bargaining.

Plea Bargaining

Plea bargaining is working with the prosecutor to come to an agreement that is fair and helpful to all. You agree to plead guilty, and the district agrees to a lower charge. This means that you may not get as harsh a sentence. But it also helps the district attorney to bring you to justice quickly and efficiently. Here, the court is not involved—only the defendant and the prosecutor. Yet, the court decides the sentence.

For example, suppose that you are arrested for selling drugs. The amount of drugs you sold might be very small. But if you are found guilty, the sentence could be harsh, even though it may even be your first offense. Once you cross the line between right and wrong, you are due a punishment.

The witness in this case is the person to whom you sold the drugs. The evidence is the drugs found on you when you were searched. The district attorney might offer to drop the charge of selling drugs and just charge you with possession of drugs. This is because it is your first offense, because you are willing to plead guilty, and because you tell the court you want to get into a drug program in order to change your behavior and build a new life. Just as intent to commit a crime is important to the courts, so is intent to improve one's behavior.

CRITICAL THINKING The Constitution says that people have a right to a jury for most crimes. Yet, because of plea bargaining, cases often do not go to trial. Do you think that a person who has not committed a crime would plead guilty and accept a plea bargain? Do you think that most guilty people would accept a plea bargain?

DID YOU KNOW? Many people are critical of plea bargaining. However, it allows the courts to save time by eliminating the long delays of trials. In this way, the criminal justice system is able to handle the huge volume of cases.

EYE OPENER According to the Statistical Abstract from 1992 of the U.S. District Court, in 1990, less than 6 percent of people arrested for homicide have been acquitted.

CRITICAL THINKING
How can talking back increase tensions and increase the possibility of an arrest taking place?

The judge does not have to accept the plea bargain. You do not have to either. People who support plea bargaining say that it is good. People plead guilty, help the system work and move along, and do not have to wait a long time for a trial. People who are against it say that too many criminals receive lighter sentences that do not really punish them. What is your opinion?

Arrest in School

What if you are arrested in school? As always, anyplace, anytime, if you think you are about to be arrested, **do not say anything until you talk with a lawyer**. If the police want to question you at school, ask them to call your parents. You can give them your name and address. It is possible that answering a few questions would not hurt you. You are the only one who knows whether you have done anything illegal. But, whether innocent or guilty, it is best to stay silent.

The police must give you the *Miranda* warning. However, the school officials are not required to. For example, if a high school principal asked a student if he had bought marijuana in school and the student said yes, this would be a confession. This confession would help convict the student. The evidence could be used in court because the school official was a private citizen. Private citizens are not required to give the *Miranda* warning.

 Workbook
Self-Check p.20
Reality-Check p.21

 TO LEARN MORE
The Peoples Guide to Government: Judicial Branch, pp. 32-33, 48

Understanding Chapter 9

1. How do you know when you are under arrest?
2. Explain how bail works.
3. What is plea bargaining?

Chapter 10

Your Lawyer and You

Ken W. and a friend, Don, were arrested for shooting and killing someone. Ken W. called his lawyer. His lawyer told the police not to question Ken unless she was there. They questioned him anyway. When witnesses were not able to identify or pick out Ken as the guilty person in a lineup, he was set free. But Don was convicted. Three years later, the police got a tape recording of Ken that tied him to the murder. Ken had not known that the tape was being made. The tape was made by Don who wanted to work with the police in order to get a reduced sentence. This evidence finally helped to convict Ken W. in court.

CHECK vocabulary words in bold. LOOK UP word meanings in the glossary beginning on page 92.

Ken W.'s lawyer appealed his case. She said that she had told the police not to question him unless she was with him. She said that Don's plan to tape Ken was just like having the police question him. She said that, just as in the beginning, the police should have called her first. The state court of appeals agreed that Ken's rights had not been protected, and a new trial was ordered.

In this chapter, you will learn about why every person who is arrested needs a lawyer at all times. Things may not be finally decided at the point of arrest or of conviction and sentencing. You will find out what a lawyer does and how you can best work with your lawyer.

CRITICAL THINKING

The arguments attorneys make, based on the evidence, often use a kind of thinking or reasoning called *logic*. Other ingredients that form part of an argument might be: custom, right, duty, fault, cause, ownership, and common sense. Why do you think it helps to use more than one kind of argument to win a case?

What Lawyers Do

A lawyer has gone to law school and knows about both federal law and state law. All lawyers have to take exams about the laws of their home state. If you are not a lawyer, you cannot know about all the different laws. Think of the criminal justice system as being a foreign country: The lawyer becomes your guide in this country because she speaks and understands the legal language.

Attorney Jameson says: "In 1873, the U.S. Supreme Court said that Myra Bradwell could not practice law because she was a woman. Instead, she started a legal newspaper and spent quarter of a century fighting for equal rights for women. I became a lawyer, knowing that there is still more to be done to create true equality for everyone in the criminal justice system — from the treatment of suspects to the appointment of Supreme Court judges."

When do you need a lawyer? You need a lawyer to represent you as soon as you are under arrest. Research shows that people who use lawyers before they go to court have a better idea of what will happen. They can have everything explained to them and are better able to make choices when necessary.

In the movies and on TV, lawyers always seem to be either in court or chasing suspects. In real life, lawyers do a lot of important paperwork in their offices. Many of them do not go to court. Every lawyer is an expert in a special part of the law. A lawyer who helps people understand laws about taxes would not be of much help to someone accused of a crime. The criminal lawyer knows a lot about criminal law and helps people who have been accused of crimes.

What can a lawyer do to help you? He can:

- try to have the charges changed or dropped
- try to have the bail changed according to what you can pay
- try to have illegal evidence suppressed or not used
- talk to witnesses and to police to help build a good case
- find out whether the prosecution has a strong or a weak case
- attend all of the hearings and act and speak for you
- help choose a fair jury
- **represent** you at the trial
- arrange plea bargain if necessary
- help you prepare for sentencing
- decide whether or not to appeal your case
- make an appeal, if necessary

What are other ways in which a lawyer can help you? Your lawyer can assist you in:

- getting a lower bail. The lawyer will ask you about your home, family, school, or job. This information will help the judge decide that you probably will not skip bail. The lawyer can tell the judge all the reasons why you should have a certain amount of bail or no bail at all.

- talking to witnesses and to the police. The lawyer will meet with witnesses and the police to discover more facts that will help your case. These facts will be told by the lawyer at the trial.

- choosing a fair jury. Your lawyer and the prosecution lawyer both want jurors who will be fair. The law says that if your lawyer does not think a juror will be fair, she can refuse to let the person serve on the jury. The prosecution can do the same for his side.

- helping you to prepare for sentencing.

- deciding when to appeal.

Choosing members of a jury can take a long time. For example, if a person being considered as a juror has been accused of shoplifting or works in a store that has problems with shoplifters, then your lawyer could not allow the juror to serve.

In helping you to prepare for sentencing, the lawyer works hard to win the case. Suppose a person is arrested for possession of drugs. Even if the evidence is enough to convict the suspect, the lawyer can talk with the suspect about entering a drug program. She could also ask people who know the suspect to write letters to the court. These letters might say why the suspect is a person who is able to change his behavior. All of this could help the judge decide to give the person a sentence that is a chance for him to change his ways rather than just a punishment.

After the trial, if a lawyer thinks that the prosecution made a lot of mistakes, then the lawyer will want to appeal. Many cases are overturned after they are appealed. This means that the suspect are granted new trials.

Finding a Lawyer

If you need a lawyer, the best way to find one is to ask your friends. If they have used a good lawyer, they will tell you. Another way is to call the **bar association**. This is an organization to which all qualified lawyers belong. It can send you a list of lawyers.

What if you cannot find a lawyer right away? Ask the police at the police station. They must find you a lawyer. There is usually a **public defender** or legal aid lawyer to help you. That lawyer can help you until you get one of your own choice. If you cannot afford a lawyer, then the public defender or legal aid lawyer will still defend you.

What should you tell your lawyer? You should tell your lawyer everything you know about the crime. Your lawyer has to have information to defend you. Anything you say to your lawyer is **privileged** or private, information. The lawyer cannot tell anyone else what you say. Yet, your lawyer has to know the truth to be able to build a good case for you. The lawyer is working for you. You and your lawyer are a team not only before the trial, but also during the trial and sentencing and after the sentencing.

CRITICAL THINKING
Why would a lawyer represent a suspect whom she thought was guilty? Why is this necessary in order for the criminal justice system to work?

DID YOU KNOW? According to the federal Administrative Office of the United States Courts, African Americans have the highest overall percentage among minority groups on the federal bench. The higher percentage of Hispanics serve as district court judges. Individuals reported as having physical challenges serve as judicial officers at all levels.

Understanding Chapter 10

1. Why do you need a lawyer in a criminal case?
2. What can a lawyer do that you cannot do for yourself?
3. How can you finding a qualified lawyer?

 Workbook
Self-Check p.22
Reality-Check p.23

 TO LEARN MORE
The Peoples Guide to Government: Guides to the Judicial Branch, pp. 34-37

Chapter 11

Trial and Sentencing

Peter K. was a college professor. In the 1960s, he was arrested as part of a **protest** at a restaurant. The protest was about the fact that the restaurant would not serve African Americans. He and a group of about seven other people sat down at the lunch counter and refused to move until they were served. The owner called the police to come and arrest the protesters. The jury in the trial could not agree on a verdict. As a result, the judge said that the trial did not count. A year later, Peter K. had not yet been tried again. Peter K. correctly went to court to fight for his right to a speedy trial.

CHECK vocabulary words in bold. LOOK UP word meanings in the glossary beginning on page 92.

The local court still did not act. Finally, the Supreme Court agreed that the Sixth Amendment gave all suspects the right to a speedy trial. Before Peter K.'s case, this right was only applied to federal cases. After Peter K.'s case, this right would be in effect for all cases.

In this chapter, you will learn about your right to a trial and your rights at the trial. You will also learn all about sentencing.

CRITICAL THINKING
Some people believe that no jury can be completely fair because the average person listens and watches the media to a degree that makes being impartial to certain kinds of crime impossible.

The Right to a Jury Trial

Do you have the right to a jury trial? Generally, a person who has been accused of a crime has a right to a trial by jury. In certain situations, you can decide to give up that right and choose to have a trial by a judge without a jury. This depends on the crime and the details of it. You should make this decision only after carefully discussing your choices with your lawyer.

Your lawyer can also decide that, for some reason, you will only be able to get a fair trial if it takes place in another city. He may think that the jurors might have made up their minds about the case even before the start of the trial. The story of the crime might have appeared on the television or on the radio.

Actress Maria P. says: "I played a defense attorney on a TV show. Soon after, I was called for jury duty. But both the defense lawyer and the district attorney refused to let me serve. They were concerned that the other jury members might forget that I was not really a defense attorney and treat me differently. Believe me, juries are selected carefully. How one person sees another in his or her mind is very important to the criminal justice system."

Do juveniles have a right to a trial? The answer is sometimes. In some states they do, and in others they do not. Some trials for juveniles are open to the public, and some are not. But accused juveniles who are to be tried in juvenile court do not ever have a jury trial. Check your state's laws on the subject. Remember that juvenile records are always private.

Your Rights at a Trial

You have six basic rights at a trial:

■ **The right to a public trial.** This means that anyone can come to see the trial. The reason is so that everyone can see the evidence. A person cannot be sent to prison with little or no evidence against her. Usually, the trial is open to the media. Reporters may attend. Some states even allow TV cameras in the courtroom.

■ **The right to a speedy trial.** Not everyone agrees on what *speedy* means. The U.S. Congress passed a law that says you have to come to trial within 100 days for a federal offense. If you do not have a trial within 100 days, the charges can be dropped. But different states have different laws. One state might say three months, while another might say one year for misdemeanors and three years for a felony. Check your state's law on this subject.

You may be in jail while waiting for a trial. However, if you are convicted, the time you already spent in jail might count toward the sentence you are given.

■ **The right to appear at the trial.** This means that if, for any reason, you are unable to come to the courtroom, the trial will be have to be delayed. There are times, however, when trials are held without the defendant. For example, defendants can become extremely upset. They may say angry words to the witnesses. The judge may have such defendants removed from the courtroom.

■ **The right to face witnesses and question them.** You or your lawyer have the right to **cross-examine** or question witnesses. You also have the right to call witnesses for your case.

■ **The right not to speak.** You do not have to testify or speak at your own trial. The district attorney cannot call you as a witness. If you choose to speak for yourself, then the district attorney can cross-examine you.

■ **The right against having to be tried twice for the same crime.** This means that you cannot stand trial or be tried twice for the same crime. This would be double jeopardy. The district attorney cannot appeal a not-guilty verdict. However, you may appeal a guilty verdict.

In Court

How should you behave in court? You may testify, or you may not. However, the jury will watch you during the trial. Your lawyer will give you advice about how to dress and act. It is a good idea to follow the advice. Be polite in the courtroom. Do not become angry at what might be said. Be a good listener.

Who can testify against you? The answer is almost anyone. Yet, there are some people who have a relationship, or link, to you. For example, what you tell your lawyer is private. Whatever is said between any two people in a relationship does not have to be told to anyone else.

A lawyer cannot tell anyone what you tell him. However, this information is only privileged if the crime has already happened. When

anyone reveals plans to do something illegal when talking with a lawyer, this information is not private.

What other special relationships can there be legally? Husbands and wives do not have to testify against each other. Also, what a husband and wife tell each other can be kept private. Yet, husbands and wives can testify against each other if they so choose. For example, if one spouse brings charges against the other in a beating case, then one partner can testify or speak about the hurt that was done by the other partner.

Religious professionals such as priests, ministers, or rabbis can also refuse to testify if suspects have told them something in private. But any time someone else besides the other person in the special relationship has also heard the private information, it is no longer private.

Finally, doctors do not have to testify. Some states also let psychiatrists and journalists refuse to testify. Check the laws in your state about privacy one special relationship.

What happens at the trial? In Chapter 4, you learned about what happens at a trial. Each side gives **testimony**, presents evidence, and calls witnesses. The judge explains the law to the jury and tells the jury what kinds of verdicts it can give. The jury then acquits or convicts the person, or says it cannot decide. If it cannot decide, it is a hung jury, and there may be another trial with another jury.

What happens after conviction? If the verdict is guilty, a person can then appeal. The appeal for state cases goes up a step to the next highest court in the state system. Federal cases go up a step to the next highest federal court. Each state has rules about reasons for appeal.

What happens while your case is on appeal? The judge can change the amount of bail or take away bail. If she thinks you would **skip bail**, then you might have to stay in jail during the appeal.

Sentencing

Sentencing usually does not take place on the day you are convicted. As the accused, you would have to return to court for sentencing. In some states, the jury sentences the defendant. In other states, the judge does the sentencing. Some states have a state office that says how long the sentence will be. Check you state's laws on this subject.

How long can prison sentences be? There are two kinds of prison sentences. Some crimes have mandatory sentences. This means the law says the crime is punished by a certain number of years in prison. The judge or jury cannot choose or change this sentence. For example, drug-related crimes have mandatory sentences in many states.

For other crimes, the judge or jury can choose the sentence. The number of years can be fixed, or not able to be changed, or the number of years can be not fixed. For example, if you are sentenced to from five to ten years, you have to serve five years at least before you can be paroled. But after that, your case can be reviewed. If you stayed out of trouble, the judge may decide that five years is enough. If you did not

The People's Publishing Group, Inc.: *Crime and the Law*

stay out of trouble, the judge may decide to make the sentence longer. This would also depend on whether or not this was your first offense.

Can you get a lighter sentence? If you have committed a serious crime or if this is not your first offense, the answer is no. In either case, you do not deserve less punishment. On the other hand, if this is your first offense and you can show that you really want to change your behavior, you might get a lighter sentence.

A probation officer makes a report to the judge before sentencing. The report tells about your behavior and what you did in the past before the crime. Your friends, your boss, and other people who know you could write letters to the court to say you want to become a lawful person.

Can you be convicted and not go to jail? If the judge thinks you are a person who can be trusted, you might receive a **suspended sentence**. This means the sentence is not carried out if you obey the judge's rules. For example, if the judge thinks you got in trouble because of the bad influence of your friends, then one rule might be that you may not see your friends. If the judge finds out that you have spent time with them, then you could go to jail.

Another way you might be convicted but not go to jail is if you are sentenced to probation. Probation is still punishment. Probation means that you have to follow certain rules in order to stay out of jail. If you break the rules of probation, you will go back to court for sentencing all over again.

When you are on probation, a probation officer supervises, or is in charge of, you. You report to him regularly. The job of the probation officer is to help you with your problems. He may help you get back into school, find an apartment, or get a job. When your probation is over, you are a free citizen. You then need to think about getting your record of conviction cleared. This depends on your state's law.

Parole

The Federal Sentencing Reform Act of 1984 eliminated, or took away, parole for felons sentenced before 1992. Those convicted before 1992 and eligible for parole were not affected. Yet, parole is still a possibility for persons convicted of other kinds of crimes.

After you have served time in prison, you might be placed on parole before your sentence is over. *Parole* means "word" in French. It means that you give your word not to commit any more crimes. A parole board decides whether or not you can be let go — whether or not you deserve to be trusted by society.

People on parole usually have to serve a certain amount of time. For example, on a life sentence, twenty-five years might have to be served before you can be given parole. The parole board does not have to give you parole.

If you are paroled, like probation, you meet with a parole officer regularly. You must also follow certain rules while on parole. For example, you will not be allowed to drink alcohol. If you break the rules,

CRITICAL THINKING The majority of suspects tried for homicide are not acquitted, but are sentenced to prison. Why do you think this is so?

DID YOU KNOW? Probation officers might have, on the average, about 200 individuals to supervise. This is according to Professor Charles Lindner, the John Jay College of Criminal Justice, New York City.

EYE OPENER There are two-and-one-half-million people on probation. They are mostly juveniles, first-time offenders.

you will go back to prison. Going back to prison means that you have failed to make a change for the better in your life even though you have been given a second change.

What happens after you are released? Each state has different rules about the rights of convicted people. In some states, for example, you may lose some of your civil rights.

You may lose the right to vote, or you may lose the right to work at certain jobs. You may also lose the right to hold public office or to serve on a jury. Yet, you may be able to get some of these rights back. Make sure you know the laws in your state.

Workbook
Self-Check p.24
Reality-Check p.25

☞ **TO LEARN MORE**

The Peoples Guide to Government:
The Judicial Branch, pp. 32-33
The Peoples Guide to: Drug Education,
pp. 38-39

Understanding Chapter 11

1. What six rights do you have at a trial?
2. Explain the two kinds of sentences you can receive.
3. Tell what happens after the verdict.

IN THIS PART YOU WILL LEARN
- define human dignity and self-respect ■ know how it feels to be a victim
- understand the importance of respecting the human dignity of others ■ identify what really happens when someone becomes a victim

Victims and Witnesses

COOPERATIVE LEARNING ACTIVITY

EMPOWER YOURSELF

Can you lose what you cannot see?

Can you imagine what it would be like to temporarily or permanently lose control over your life, where you actually lost the ability to live your everyday life the way you had been used to doing? Explore with your small group the scene below that describes just such a situation.

The Scene: Three youths walk down a dark street looking for trouble. They see a lady on her way home from work. They smile at each other and then jump in front of her, shrieking and flashing knives, to scare her to death. She screams in horror, unable to take another step. The youths walk way, laughing, taking nothing, but pleased with themselves. She makes her way to a restaurant and begins to get chest pains.

What makes a victim a victim?

1. Have you ever heard about where one person insulted or tried to do harm against another person? Perhaps on the news? Discuss the effects this could have on a person's life.

2. Look at the following list of words. Place them in groups by writing them in large circles on a piece of art paper. Make sure each person in the group laces at least one word in each of the groups. You will probably have two to four circles.
   Money, clothing, your life, feeling of security, peace of mind, jewelry, confidence, control over things that happen to you, guilt, motor vehicle, physical health and well-being, emotional health and well-being, fear, anxiety, embarrassment, self-respect.

3. Next, label the word groups by writing why the items were placed in each group (what they have in common). Write a statement that draws a conclusion about them on the blackboard. Participate in a class discussion on what the groups and labels might have to do with the story.

4. Compare your word group with those of others. Make a list of things a victim can lose that you can see. Then make a list of things a victim can lose that you cannot see. Labels these lists: *visible* and *invisible.*

5. Now look at the original list of words and write down only the words that are about feelings and how people think of themselves. Are they positive? negative? Discuss this in the group and make a list of positive feeling words. Change the negative one already in the list to positive, and add them to the list.

While reading this chapter...
Stop and think about how important human dignity is to everyone, no matter what their background story might be.

Chapter 12

Be a Crime Buster

Kate J. came home from work at 3:20 A.M. She parked her car some distance from her apartment house. As she walked toward her house, a man attacked her. She screamed loudly and struggled to get away. The whole block could hear her cries for help.

CHECK vocabulary words in bold. LOOK UP word meanings in the glossary beginning on page 92.

CRITICAL THINKING
How easy or difficult do you think it would be to identify a suspect, even a few days after the crime?

Officer Perkins says: "Often a crime will happen on a crowded street, but we cannot find a single witness. They disappear into the woodwork because they do not want to get involved. The excuse is that someone else will report it. It is up to everyone to help catch criminals. The next victim might be a friend, a relative, or even you."

Kate J. eventually died from her injuries. The attacker disappeared and was never brought to justice. People in the community promised themselves that they would not let this happen again. However, it was too late for Kate J.

In this chapter, you will find out why reporting crime is necessary. It will describe how you can be a crimebuster. It will also tell how you can help the victim.

Why Report Crime?

The faster a crime is reported, the better the chance is of solving it. If you are a victim, call the police right away. If you are a witness, call the police right away. This helps the police to catch the suspect. Even if the crime has already happened, you should still report it quickly. There are five important reasons for doing this:

1. You may be able to get your property back. If the police know what was stolen, they might be able to find it.
2. If the crime was violent, some states will pay your doctor bills and for stolen property, but only if there is a police report.
3. A **police report** is a legal record. If you have insurance to pay for stolen property, you need a police report.
4. If you report the loss of property on your income tax, you need a police report.
5. You will be helping others. The police need to know where the high-crime areas are. They need to know the suspects to be

looking for. Crime reports help them see crime patterns in neighborhoods. For example, if they see that a lot of crime is happening on a particular street, they can put more police there to make it safer for everyone-for your grandparents, parents, sisters, brothers, and friends, too.

CRITICAL THINKING
About half of all felonies and two-thirds of all larcenies are not reported. Why do you think people do not report crimes? Do you think there are any good reasons not to?

How To Report Crime

If you see a crime happening, call the police emergency number (dial 911) or the phone operator (dial 0). This may seem simple to do. Believe it or not, however, many people do not call because they think that someone else has. As a result, nobody calls.

What should you tell the police when you call? You should tell them:

1. where the crime is happening
2. what you remember about the suspect
3. information about any car or vehicle involved
4. if anyone is hurt
5. as much as you can about everything else

Everything you remember can be important. Also, you need to tell the police your name and where you are located because they will need your help as a witness. If you are in a safe place, stay there. If you cannot wait until the police come, give this information to another witness so you can be called. You can also call the police station later. Remember: someday you could be the victim in need of someone to call the police. It could save your life.

DID YOU KNOW? Crime Stoppers is an organization in the United States and Canada that promotes crimebusting. It gives rewards to citizens who give information that help solve crimes.

Helping Victims

How can you help the victim? Help the victim by calling the police right away. Wait with the victim until the police arrive. Do not move the victim. Give first aid only if you know what you are doing. There may be other people watching who know first aid. Ask if anyone is a doctor or has medical knowledge.

Ask the victim if there is a friend or relative you can call. Then call that person and tell where the victim is. Tell which hospital the victim is being taken to. Help the victim pick up or collect personal property.

When is it *not* a good idea to be helpful? If you see the crime happening, often you can help. Yet, there are some times when it can be dangerous. It is important to try to tell the difference.

For example, never let a stranger into your apartment. It usually is a trick. The person may say she was robbed or was in an accident and needs to use the phone. If you let the person in, you may very well become a victim. As long as you did not actually see a crime or an accident happen, do not open the door. Instead, tell the person you will call for help. The same kind of situation can happen on the street.

Sometimes, there are clues to danger. For example, Steve, a cab

EYE OPENER About 40 percent of robberies and 36 percent of assaults on teenagers happen in schools. Burglaries happen in schools five times more often than in places of business. The climate of violence in schools can make it difficult for students to learn.

CRITICAL THINKING
Why would remembering many details about only one of several suspects be enough to help solve a crime?

driver, had to come to a sudden stop. Two men had stepped into the road, blocking him. They came over to the window and asked to use his radio so that they could call for help. They said that a friend was hurt. Steve saw that there was a pay phone on the corner. He also was sure everyone knew that yellow cabs did not have two-way radios. So he stepped on the gas and drove away from danger.

If you do not actually see the crime happen, do not even get close to the person who is supposed to be the victim. Offer to call the police, but do not offer any other help. Keep yourself out of danger.

How can you remember what you saw? When you are a crime witness, the police will need to ask you a lot of questions. But many people forget what they saw because they became frightened. Try to remember the following things about the suspect: height, weight, age, coloring (hair, skin, eyes), any special features like scars or tattoos, and the kind of clothing or jewelry worn. If there is more than one suspect, try to remember these things about at least one of them.

If there was a car or other vehicle involved, try to remember the color, make, and model, as well as the license plate. The state and number on the license plate are very important. Even a few numbers can help. If you are the victim, give the police a list of what was taken. It will become part of the police record.

DID YOU KNOW? In many large cities, citizens can bust crimes by being on the lookout for scams. Scans involve fooling or tricking the public to commit a crime. Often, criminals work their scams, or criminal plans, in pairs or small groups. For example, the scam might be a fake accident to cause the intended victim to act in a careless manner.

Getting Involved

Should You Try to Stop a Crime Yourself? It is hard to know whether you should try to stop a crime. Every situation is different. You have to judge how dangerous it would be to try. Most people want to help, but are afraid to act alone. They should be. Sometimes, a group can chase and capture a suspect, but only if they are sure that the suspect is not carrying a weapon.

For example, a suspect grabbed a purse from a woman. When she screamed, people on the block blew their whistles. Several people came out of their houses to chase the suspect. The suspect pulled out a knife; people were afraid to grab him. Still, a group chased him down the street while others called the police.

Next, the suspect ran into a building. The crowd stayed outside. The police arrived and the suspect, who was on the roof, was arrested. The police thanked everyone on this block for working together to help stop the crime.

Another example of a person who safely helped a victim is Anita. She was standing in line for the bus. When it arrived, people crowded to get on. Anita saw a man reach into a woman's purse and take out her wallet. "What are you doing?" Anita yelled. The man dropped the wallet and ran. Sometimes, it is enough to yell and frighten the person.

Citizen's Arrest

Can you ever arrest a suspect? The answer is yes. This is called a **citizen's arrest**, or an arrest by someone who is not a police officer.

EYE OPENER There has been a recent pattern of taxi-driver killings in a large city—one almost every seven to ten days. Unfortunately, in special situations when the crime is committed in a physically isolated place like the inside of a taxicab, it becomes very difficult for a crimebuster to become involved.

The People's Publishing Group, Inc.: *Crime and the Law*

All private citizens have the right to arrest someone. In this respect, all citizens help to police society.

A citizen's arrest means holding someone until the police arrive. This can also mean taking the person to the police station. Yet, you should be careful not to put yourself in danger.

Most police rarely do unlawful things. But it can happen. If you ever witness the police doing something you think might be illegal, remember their badge numbers and report them. Get names and addresses of any other witness(es), just as you would for any other crime situation or for any other suspect.

CRITICAL THINKING
If you become a crimebuster, what do you have to gain? If you do not get involved when it would be safe to do so, what do you have to lose?

DID YOU KNOW? Most people can remember seven facts or bits of information for a short period of time, but no more. Any information in addition to the seven items might not be remembered or might be reported inaccurately.

Understanding Chapter 12

1. Why is it important to be a crimebuster?
2. If you witness a crime, what information should you try to remember?
3. How can you help a crime victim?

 Workbook
Self-Check p.26
Reality-Check p.27

Chapter 13

Tell What You Know

John H. worked in a building downtown. He never spoke to his neighbors down the hall, but noticed lots of unfriendly looking individuals coming and going at all hours when he was working late. Then, one night, he heard gunfire. He walked down the hall and saw a man with a gun pursuing another, who was bleeding badly, down the stairs. The next minute, a group of men rushed downstairs, too. John ran to the window and witnessed more gunplay. When the police came, John told them everything he had seen. Because the suspects belonged to a famous crime organization, the court ordered protection for John.

CHECK vocabulary words in bold. LOOK UP word meanings in the glossary beginning on page 92.

CRITICAL THINKING
Why do you think that the law says that a husband and wife usually have the right not to have to testify against each other?

Witness Lisa H. says: "The crime I had witnessed involved one of the biggest drug deals of the decade. Because of my testimony as a witness, several key players in two rival crime organizations are now behind bars. Sure, I had to move. But I would do it all over again if I had to."

After he received threats on the phone, the government decided to play it safe and help John move to another town to start a new life. Better safe than sorry. John felt good about having done what was right. He also felt satisfied that the government was behind him all the way.

In this chapter, you will learn what a witness does. You will learn about what to do in court as a witness.

Witnesses

What kinds of witnesses are there? A witness is a person who can give a personal description of something. There are three kinds of witnesses.

The first kind is a police officer who witnessed the crime or talked to the victim.

The second kind of witness is an ordinary citizen who knows something about the crime. She may have seen or heard something about the crime. This witness can only testify about something she has seen, touched, smelled, felt, or tasted. For example, a witness in a poisoning case might testify that the suspect gave her food that smelled funny, and that because of this, she did not eat it. However, another person might have taken food from the suspect and gotten very sick, or even worse.

The third kind of witness is an **expert witness.** This is a witness who did not actually see the crime, but who does know a lot about something that is part of the crime. For example, an expert on guns could say whether he thought a bullet could have been fired from a roof or from the ground. Many expert witnesses are scientists.

What happens after you witness a crime? If the police arrive soon after the crime, they may take witnesses along while they look for the suspects. If the police catch the suspects, they may take witnesses to the police station to identify them.

You are asked to look at a lineup. You should try to remember the details about the suspect. If the lineup happens right after the crime, the suspect will probably still be wearing the same clothes. If the lineup is a day or two later, the suspect will have different clothes. The suspect may even have shaved or changed hair style. If you are not sure that someone in the lineup is the suspect, you need to say so. Always tell the truth. Never guess. If you do not guess correctly, the wrong person may be convicted.

The police have not yet arrested anyone. They may then ask you to look through some photographs of people who had been arrested before. If the person you saw had never been arrested, the picture will not be found. In this situation, you might be able to describe the person to a police artist.

The artist would then draw a picture from what you say. Artists often use computers to make their drawings. The picture might be handed out to police officers to help them recognize the suspect, or it can be posted around the neighborhood.

What happens after you identify the suspect? Once a suspect has been identified, you will meet with a lawyer from the district attorney's office. Tell her what happened.

At a preliminary hearing, a day or two later, the district attorney will give the evidence to the court. The court will decide whether there is enough evidence to bring the suspect to trial. You will have to testify at this hearing.

The court may give the case to a **grand jury**. The grand jury will look at evidence and decide whether or not to indict or charge the suspect with the crime. If you have to give evidence to a grand jury, you will do so in secret. What you say will be private. There may be other hearings for you to attend. The court will send you notice if you must appear.

Many cases never go to trial because there is not enough evidence. Cases may sometimes be plea-bargained. However, if the case goes to trial, you will also have to testify at the trial.

Subpoenas

What should you do if you get a subpoena? A **subpoena** is a paper that says you are being called as a witness. It tells you when to come to court. You must appear if you get a subpoena because you must testify or tell what you know.

All witnesses get subpoenas. You may not have seen the crime. However, the suspect may want you to be what is called a **character witness.** A character witness testifies that the suspect has a good character. A character witness might be a teacher, an employer, or a minister.

The People's Publishing Group, Inc.: *Crime and the Law*

CRITICAL THINKING
The law says that employers must pay people for time they miss from work in order to serve on a jury. Yet, employers do not have to pay people for the time miss from work in order to be a witness. Why do you think this is so? What do you think a professional witness is?

DID YOU KNOW? Newspaper reporters often refuse to give the names of people to whom they have spoken. The Supreme Court has said that what a person says to a reporter is not private. Reporters argue that no one will talk to them if the law requires them to testify. What is your opinion?

EYE OPENER More than 75 percent of victims in one study were not bothered in any way by the defendants or defendants' relatives. This means that the possibility of a threat to a victim is not enough to stop him from telling what he knows.

If you are a witness for the state, the district attorney will review the testimony with you. If you are a witness for the defense, then the defense lawyer will do the review. If a lawyer from the other side wants to talk with you, you may want the lawyer for your side to be with you.

Does being a witness take a lot of time? The answer is that it can. There will be hearings to attend and perhaps a trial. Some courts have a telephone alert system to call you only when it is almost your turn to go to the courthouse.

Who pays for witness expenses? If you have to miss time from work to be a witness and find child-care in order to go to court, some courts provide child-care programs. Many states also have Victim/ Witness Assistance Programs. Check if there are programs in your state.

What Is a Victim/Witness Assistance Program? It is a program that helps victims and witnesses do their job. For example, it may be able to pay some of the costs you will face. People from the program can arrange with your employer for you to take time off from work and, perhaps, to get paid while you are in court.

The law says that witnesses have to get a witness fee. This is a very small amount of money. However, ask about how to be in the programs that help you financially if you are a witness.

Telling What You Know in Court

When it is time to tell your story in court, you will wait outside the courtroom until your turn. You will be called in and the court clerk will swear you in. When you are sworn in, you will be asked to raise your right hand and promise to tell the truth, the whole truth, and nothing but the truth. This is a very serious promise.

Make sure you know these five important things to remember about being a witness:

1. Show **respect** for the court: don't smoke, eat, or chew gum in the courtroom; be polite—always call the judge "Your Honor."

2. Tell the truth: Stick to the facts—tell only what you know for certain. If you do not know an answer, say so. Never guess. Speak clearly. If you need an interpreter, the court will provide one. If you are interpreter for a someone else, answer as carefully as if you were the witness.

3. Answer only the question being asked. For instance, if the lawyer asks whether you were at the laundromat on the afternoon of the crime, say yes or no. Do not say, "No, but I was there that morning." If you give information that is not asked for, it might hurt or confuse the case.

4. Try to relax and stay calm: Never become angry. The cross-examination can be difficult. This is the time when the lawyer from the other side asks you questions. This lawyer will try to find out whether you are sure about what you witnessed. Stay calm. Do not give smart answers or make jokes. Try to show as much respect for the lawyer as possible.

The People's Publishing Group, Inc.: *Crime and the Law*

5. Pause before answering a question. When you are being cross-examined by the other side, the lawyer from your side has the chance to object to a question being asked or to complain that the question is not fair. Wait for the judge to say whether or not to answer the question.

Can you commit a crime as a witness? The answer is yes. You can break the law even as a witness. If called to testify, you must appear in court. If you refuse, you can be charged with **contempt of court,** or with not obeying or with not showing respect for the court. In some situations, you can be fined or even sent to jail.

If you tell a lie after you have promised to tell the truth, you will have committed a crime. The crime is called *perjury*. The sentence for perjury is much harsher than the sentence for contempt.

Do you always have to testify? You do not have to testify against your husband or wife if you choose not to. You also do not have to say anything against yourself in court. On the other hand, if you testify to a grand jury, you have to tell everything. The grand jury usually cannot indict or charge you with the crime by using the evidence you give in your testimony.

What if you are threatened by the suspect? The accused or the family of the accused sometimes threaten a witness. Threats do not usually happen, but they are against the law. You should report any threats to the police. They can help you get a court order to stop the threats. The police can also go with you to and from court to keep you safe. You can also ask someone from a Victim/Witness Assistance program to go with you.

CRITICAL THINKING
Why is it important to tell only what you know as fact or observation and nothing from personal opinion or guessing?

DID YOU KNOW? Being a witness is both a right and a responsibility.

Understanding Chapter 13

1. Name different ways of identifying a suspect.
2. Describe what a subpoena is.
3. What should you do if threatened either by the accused or by his/or her family?

 Workbook
Self-Check p.28
Reality-Check p.29

Chapter 14

Victims Have Rights, Too!

It has been almost a year since that day. But Lucy M.'s eyes still fill with tears when she describes what three criminals did to her home. A friend had called her at her aunt's house to tell her there had been a break-in. She rushed home to find overturned furniture, emptied drawers, broken picture frames, and her VCR, bicycle, and camera gone. The burglars had even used the microwave oven as a toilet. Lucy told police she felt as if she had been raped. The only thing not ruined were the clothes on her back.

CHECK vocabulary words in bold. LOOK UP word meanings in the glossary beginning on page 92.

CRITICAL THINKING
Some people think it is a good idea to have criminals pay back the victim. People who are against this idea say that many criminals are too poor to pay. What do you think?

Offender Jane H., says: "I shot a friend dead in a fight. I am behind bars for twenty years. I know that the victim's mother has become an advocate for victims' rights. She misses her son every day and is filled with hate when thinking of me. In just three seconds, I ruined my whole life and the lives of many others. I feel strongly that victims have rights, too."

Lucy could not sleep for days. Her emotions went from guilt and fear to anger. She closed herself off from the world and stayed home for weeks. Her bills became too high to handle, she lost her job, and she had to move in with her parents. Perhaps the worst thing is that Lucy is now afraid to leave her parents' home for fear that it will be broken into. She also has terrible nightmares. The one lucky thing is that the crime brought out the best in her friends and in her community. They raised $5,000 to help her replace the things in her life.

In this chapter, you will find out about the feelings many crime victims have. You will learn about what family and friends can do to help. You will also find out about a victim's rights.

Victims' Feelings

A crime victim feels many different feelings. These feelings can last for months or years after the crime. For example, the victim sometimes thinks that the crime was his or her fault. The victim might think, "I should have left my house earlier and not walked down that street," or "I should have run faster or fought back." The victim can feel this way even if there was nothing he could have done to prevent the crime.

If the victim's house was broken into, the victim, like Lucy, will likely feel afraid that the burglar might come back. The victim might also feel angry at having felt so helpless. Some of the victim's feelings will not be unlike the person returning home after being in a war zone.

Help for Victims

How can family and friends help a victim? Friends and family can help a victim a lot. They can stay with the victim when he or she is afraid to be alone. They can listen while the victim talks about feelings and about the crime.

Can victims get paid back what they have lost? The answer is sometimes. There are four different ways victims can get paid back, or get **restitution**, for what has been taken from them.

1. Being paid back for damage, loss, or injury: The criminal must sometimes pay money to the victim for damage or injury. For example, if someone is convicted of stealing $30, part of the person's sentence will be to pay back the $30 to the victim.

The judge may sentence a person to pay something to the community. For example, if some people are found guilty of vandalism or damaging property in a park, the judge might sentence them to clean up the park every Saturday for a year.

2. Getting money from the government for damage, loss, or injury: Some states have an office or board that pays **compensation**, or money for medical expenses, to victims of violent crimes. Other states also pay for loss of property. Still other states give money to help people who are hurt as a result of coming to the aid of a victim.

To get this kind of help, a victim needs to fill out a form and give the following information: details of the crime, names and addresses of any witness(es), the number of the police department complaint report, copies of medical bills, and the name and badge number of the police officer who wrote the crime report.

o Victims may have to report the crime within a certain amount of time. It may be a month. It may be only two days. Check what the laws are in your state.

3. Taking the criminal to a special court called the small claims court: Victims do not always need a lawyer for this kind of court.

4. Taking someone to court who, in some way, helped make it possible for the crime to happen: A victim may be able to sue someone else for damages.

For example, Kim Y.'s apartment was robbed, but the thief was not caught. Kim Y. sued his landlord in court because the lock on his door was not safe. He had complained about it many times, but his landlord had not fixed it. The landlord had not done his job. In this way, the landlord was responsible for the break-in. Kim Y. won the case, and the landlord had to fix the door as well as pay the all of the damages.

What do Victim/Witness Assistance Programs do to help? Many victims need help in dealing with their feelings about the crime.

Counseling can be the best remedy. A social worker or a person who is trained in mental health can counsel or help victims and witnesses to feel better by listening to them. This listening helps people to understand their feelings better.

The People's Publishing Group, Inc.: *Crime and the Law*

CRITICAL THINKING In the story at the beginning of this chapter, Lucy M. felt that victims have to live with the feeling of being a victim for the rest of their lives. Why do you think this is so?

HAVE YOU SEEN THIS CHILD?

REPORT ANY INFORMATION TO OUR HOTLINE

DID YOU KNOW? John Walsh is the host of a television show about crime in America. His own six-year-old son, Adam, was murdered in 1981. The murderer was never caught. Walsh found that the police had no system for keeping track of missing-children reports. He worked to have Congress pass the Missing Children's Assistance Act. Today, handbills like the above advertised the search for missing children.

EYE OPENER By giving information about criminals not yet caught, the TV show hosted by John Walsh has caused 243 criminals to be captured in five years! John Walsh also helped to make television movies about Adam and about missing children. As a result of one show, 65 missing children were found.

CRITICAL THINKING
How can sending victims to jails regularly to talk with prisoners help offenders to understand their responsibility in committing crimes?

In the example of Jenny J., she and her two children were attacked in front of a store. A teenage girl had thrown a soda can at them and Jenny J. complained. Then the girl and some friends threw Jenny to the ground. She was injured. The children had screamed in terror, but nobody came to help. Jenny finally managed to call a friend to come and get the children. She also called an ambulance.

Jenny was angry at the attackers, and she was angry because no one had helped her. This caused her to yell at her children. She went to Victim Services and asked to talk to a counselor. This helped Jenny to stop feeling upset.

An assistance program can also help victims like Jenny J. with child care while they either go to court or go to see doctors and counselors. Such programs can help victims replace lost welfare or Medicaid cards. The program may even help victims get new locks on doors!

What if there is no assistance program in your area? If there are no such programs in your area, there are other places to get help when you need it. There might be a help hotline in town. This means the victim can call a certain number and ask where to get counseling and other help. Some places have special hotlines for certain crimes. A neighborhood center may also be able to help.

What if your money or property was stolen? The police always make a list of stolen property or money. If these things are found, the police will still keep them for a while to be used as evidence. They are returned to the owner when the case is closed.

DID YOU KNOW? A very popular singer was the victim of an attack one night at a hotel. The attacker broke into her room and raped her He was never caught. The victim sued the motel, saying that the sliding glass doors of her room did not have a proper lock. The singer won the case. This was one of the first cases in which a victim got the right to protection.

Victims' Rights

Is there a bill of rights for victims? The Bill of Rights protects the rights of all the people in the United States. This set of rights was added to the Constitution. Yet, there is no bill of rights for victims in the Constitution.

In the last few years, victims' rights organizations have worked hard to make laws more fair for victims. Some states have victims' rights laws and some states do not. Check the laws in your state.

Some important rights of victims of crime are:
1. the right to be told what finally happens with the case
2. the right to be told a court hearing has been canceled
3. the right to be protected from threats
4. the right to be told about how to receive witness fees
5. the right to be given a safe area that is away from the suspect to wait in before the trial
6. the right to have property returned quickly. If possible, pictures should be taken of the property. Property should be returned ten days after photos are taken.
7. the right to have someone tell the victim's employer not to allow the victim to lose too much employment money while in court.

EYE OPENER The U.S. Department of Justice reports that one in four households was victimized by crime in 1991.

The People's Publishing Group, Inc.: *Crime and the Law*

All of these rights are for victims, witnesses, and families of victims. Victims have a right to know about everything available to help them balance the harm that has been done to them.

Can victims help themselves? Does a victim ever stop having bad feelings about the crime after it happens? The answer is often no. Yet, victims can feel stronger and better if they do something positive—like fighting back.

Fighting back does not mean going after the suspect yourself. This is always a mistake. You can be hurt or lose your life by doing so! You can help the police by trying to get evidence. It also helps if you act as a witness to make sure the suspect is convicted.

Victims who do these things also help other people from becoming victims of the same person who hurt you. Victims can help society as well as be helped by it after a crime has been committed.

CRITICAL THINKING
Relatives of victims sometimes feel that they want revenge, or to get even. But if this means committing more violence, then the harm caused by crime just continues. What can families of victims do to help themselves?

Understanding Chapter 14

1. How can you help a friend or relative who has been a victim?
2. Can a victim be paid back for loss or damages?
3. What is the victims' bill of rights?

Workbook
Self-Check p.30
Reality-Check p.31

Chapter 15

Sex Crimes

Joel V. drank a case of beer one night. He lost control of his behavior. He broke into a woman's apartment and held a knife in front of her. He said he wanted to have sex with her. The woman was afraid he would murder her. She had to give in but asked him to wear a condom. She was afraid of catching a disease and of becoming pregnant. After he left her house, she called the police. They caught him nearby.

CHECK vocabulary words in bold. LOOK UP word meanings in the glossary beginning on page 92.

CRITICAL THINKING
Some radio stations play music that talks about hurting people, drugs and violence against society. In the United States, this is called "gangsta rap." What influence can this have on the behavior of young people?

 Attorney Diaz says: "Every case is different. If you decide to fight back, you could be hurt, but this is better than being raped. If a weapon is used, especially a gun, *not* fighting back is smart. Then the most important thing becomes surviving the crime of rape, not dying."

A grand jury indicted Joel V. on **sexual assault** and burglary charges. The jury found Joel V. guilty of rape. He is now behind bars, and the woman is getting counseling help. In this chapter, you will learn about rape and **sexual harassment**. You will learn what they are and what you can do if you are raped or sexually **harassed**. You will also find out about what takes place at a rape trial.

Rape

What does the law say about rape? Rape is a crime of assault. The law says that there are two kinds of rape. One kind is forcible rape. Another kind is statutory rape.

Forcible rape is the forcing of a person to have sex. Statutory rape is having sex with a person who is too young to say yes legally. In this situation, whether the young person was forced to have sex or not, a crime was committed.

What should you do if you are raped? There are six things you must do, and do quickly, if you are raped. Read these over until you have memorized them.

1. Tell someone right away. It is best to tell an adult person you know. If you are at home, tell a neighbor. If it happens in the street, you may have to get help from a stranger. Go to a store or a restaurant. Ask to use a telephone. Tell someone everything that happened while you still remember details. If you are a woman, you may feel more comfortable talking to another woman. If you are a man, you may want to talk with a man.

2. Next, call the police. Some cities have special phone numbers for rape victims called **Rape Crisis Hotlines.** A victim can call that number or call the police emergency number.

3. Next, call the friend you told about the rape to come and be with you. A friend can help you talk to the police. A friend can help you at the hospital. Do not be afraid to show your upset feelings.

4. Next, do not answer any questions about your sex life. The police may ask you about your sex life, but you do not have to answer. You will probably be too upset to talk. You need to tell them this. Many rapes are committed by people who actually know their victims. The police may ask the victim whether he or she ever had sex with the suspect before. That is their job.

Yet, you do not have to answer this type of question. The crime of rape has nothing to do with your past or even with the day before you were assaulted. Having had sex with others before does not mean you said yes this time.

5. Next, go to the hospital. Ask the police to take you to the hospital, or go with a friend. It is very important to go to the hospital as soon as possible. You will need to have proof that you were raped. The hospital exam record will show that you were attacked. It will tell whether you have cuts or bruises.

6. Finally, do not wash anything before you go to the hospital! Many victims want to wash their body or their clothes right away. However, this would mean washing away evidence. This evidence could be hair or blood or semen from the attacker. It is also important to go to the hospital in case you have also been hurt from a struggle with the attacker.

There may be a chance that the rape causes you to become pregnant. The doctor can give you a pill to stop the pregnancy just in case. If you are in a hospital that does not give such a pill, go to a family-planning or abortion clinic as soon as possible.

Some people do not want to take this type of pill for religious or other reasons or because it can make you sick. Always ask the doctor about how any medicine might make you feel.

Can you catch a disease from being raped? The answer is yes! There are more than twenty such diseases! These are called **sexually transmitted diseases,** or **STD's**. This means that you only get them from having sex with someone who has them.

At the hospital, doctors can give you a shot to protect against many but not all of these diseases. You will need to go back to the hospital in a few weeks for tests to make sure you did not catch anything. This is important because some of the STD's have no **symptoms,** or signs. Some STD's can be caught very easily.

AIDS

Can you catch AIDS from a rapist? The answer is yes! It is possible to catch this killer disease from having sex just once with

Should you fight?   Should you run?

Should you scream? Should you give in?

CRITICAL THINKING
If you are physically threatened, don't be nice. Should you fight? Should you run? Should you scream? Should you give in to avoid being beaten or killed?

DID YOU KNOW? Ten out of seventeen men said that if the women they had tried to rape had run, screamed, or fought, they might have avoided the rape. Yet, these suspects did not mean crying, begging, or making a deal.

EYE OPENER The crime of rape happens five times more often in the United States than in Germany, thirteen times more than in England, and twenty times more than in Japan.

another person. You cannot know for sure if you have caught it until a long time after the attack. It often takes years before the AIDS virus shows up in a blood test.

AIDS is the most serious disease of the century. After being raped, a person must be tested as soon he or she arrives at the hospital. It is a matter of life and death. It is not something that can only happen to other people. If a person is casual or not careful about sex, he or she is playing with death. Until a person knows the test result, he or she must take care not to infect another person, just in case.

Some of the Feelings Rape Victims Have

Rape victims have many of the same feelings as other crime victims. They may feel frightened, depressed, or sad. They may even feel guilty and need help to know that the rape was not their fault.

Rape victims also need help to learn how to protect themselves. They need to learn how to feel safe again. They need to talk about what happened and need a lot of support from friends and family.

Where can the rape victim get help? He or she can go to a special place or center that helps rape victims with medical and emotional problems.

Rape Victim Pressing Charges

Many rapes are committed by people who know their victims, even if not well. This means that the victim can often identify the attacker for the police. Yet, believe it or not, victims sometimes do not press charges because they are embarrassed or frightened. This is definitely wrong .

It is the right thing to go to the police. Rape is a terrible crime. The police and courts have a better understanding of how rape victims feel than in the past. However, rape trials are still very hard emotionally on the victims.

What happens at a rape trial? At a rape trial, the victim has to tell the story once again. The suspect's lawyer may turn things around and try to find anything the victim might have said or done to make the victim seem guilty.

For example, if the victim asks the rapist to wear a condom and even supplies one for safety, the defense lawyer might say that it is possible the victim was agreeing to have sex. To make sure things are not turned around, the victim must show honesty. This is the best way of answering uncomfortable questions.

Remember, too, that the law tries to treat everyone the same. This means that the suspect's past sex life cannot be brought up, even if he or she was tried for rape before. Also, be prepared to be asked: "Did you not know better than to go on that dangerous street alone?" or "Didn't you know better than to open the door to a stranger?" The court will need to ask these questions to make sure that you had nothing to do with causing the attack. And, of course, while it is a mistake to take such risks, it is not a reason to be raped. Rape is still a crime, and you, as a victim are still not guilty.

The People's Publishing Group, Inc.: *Crime and the Law*

The Right Thing to Do

Did you resist? To resist means to try to stop something from happening to you. The law says rape is sex without the consent of the victim. Many people think, then, that this means the victim must fight and struggle. This is always smart. If you think however that struggling, kicking, or screaming might make the attacker hurt you even more, then it is not smarter to resist. Every person needs to do what is best to save his or her life. Every attack is different. Every attacker is different.

A person needs to decide what to do at the moment of the attack, and very quickly. The fear of being murdered can make a person not struggle. The person who does not struggle is still a victim 100 percent. Fear does not equal consent.

Is there a witness to the rape? If there are no witnesses and you have no cuts and bruises, it will be harder to prove there was a rape. This is why it is so important for you to tell someone right after it happens. Even though this person did not witness the rape, the person did witness how upset you were right after the crime happened.

Did you know the suspect? Rape victims often know their attacker. For example, there was a case of a woman who was raped by someone delivering food to her apartment. Another person was raped by the building's security guard. The rapist could even be a jealous friend. This does not mean you need to worry about every person you see. But it does mean that you must be careful always.

How careful should you be? There are some simple rules everyone should follow

- Never let a complete stranger into your house.

- Be careful about allowing even a friend of a friend to come into your home alone.

Date Rape

What about dates and parties? These kinds of situations are times when a kind of rape called **date rape** can happen. If, for example, you go out on a date with someone who wants to have sex, and you do not, you need to know how to protect yourself. A victim of date rape has a hard time proving the rape in court because the victim started out by agreeing to go on a date.

Remember that saying yes to a date or a dance is not the same as saying yes to sex.

Many times, victims are raped at parties because everyone is drinking. Sometimes, people even faint. Also, women usually are not physically able, because of their size, to drink as much as men without feeling drunk. When a person is feeling faint, he or she cannot really know what is happening. As a result, he or she may not even remember being raped.

What can you do to avoid date rape? The best thing to do is to keep physical control of yourself. This means to never drink too much at parties. Never drink if you are under age. Also, do not choose to attend

CRITICAL THINKING People who have been the victims of rape often say that they will never be the same. Why do you think this is so?

DID YOU KNOW? If a person does not say *yes* to sex, this is the same as saying no.

EYE OPENER Today, although only 3 to 10 percent of all rapes are reported each year, this more than in the past.

parties that have no one supervising them. Do not go to parties where you do not know most of the people very well.

Believe it or not, rape is never OK, even in a party or date situation. Criminal behavior is illegal and wrong all the time. It doesn't matter what anyone else thinks: you can have control over your own behavior. You know what is wrong and what is right. If you have been date raped, you need to press charges.

Can you be raped by your spouse? In the past, most state laws said no. Most states said that it is more important that a spouse have the right to have sex with his or her partner. However, more and more states are now changing their laws. People are realizing that the rights of a person not to have sex should always be protected.

Sex needs two people who agree every time, not just some of the time. Otherwise, a rape has taken place.

We understand that many rapists rape again. Their behavior becomes a pattern. That is why a victim who can put a rapist in jail will be helping to save other people from this violent crime.

Sexual Harassment

What is sexual harassment? Sexual harassment happens any time one person touches another person's body, talks about sex to them in an unwelcome way, or looks at your body in a way that makes you upset. It can be your boss saying you must have sex if you want to keep your job. It can be a classmate making jokes about private parts of your body.

Where does sexual harassment happen? It happens almost everywhere. It is a growing problem in workplaces and in schools. A student who has been harassed, may have a problem about wanting to return to school.

Is sexual harassment against the law? In many cases, sexual harassment is a criminal act. It is definitely against the law for an employer to demand sex so that you can keep your job. Although you cannot usually have someone sent to jail for sexual harassment, you can certainly bring charges against the person. If the person is found guilty, he or she may have to pay a fine. A fine is a punishment, too. For example, one man brought charges against his female boss. He said she had bothered him for six years. He won the case.

What if sexual harassment happens in school? Does your school have a way to handle people who commit sexual harassment? If it does, find out what it is. If it does not, here are some things that you and your friends can do:

■ If anyone at school (a teacher, a student, or a security guard) is harassing you, tell that person what you are feeling and that you want the person to stop.

■ If the person does not stop, then go to someone above that person, perhaps the principal or a school counselor, with a list of things that happened. The list should say what, when, where, and who. Also,

The People's Publishing Group, Inc.: *Crime and the Law*

list the names of any witnesses. List what you said or did to the harasser and what the harasser said or did to you. Finally, don't forget to say how you felt about the harassment.

■ If the harassment happens again, go to someone on an even higher level, such as a school-board member or the superintendent of schools. Continue to keep track of the dates, times, and witnesses to the harassment. You cannot report on the crime if you do not keep a record like a reporter.

For example, a student was very upset because people were writing sexual things about her on the school bathroom walls. She complained to the principal. The school did not even wash the walls. It was as if they did not care that she felt harmed emotionally.

The student sued the school and won her case. The court said that the school had to do something to stop the harassment. Sexual harassment is different from rape. It can be physical or just emotional. But it can include everything short of rape.

Today, people convicted on sexual harassment do not get prison sentences. Yet, the laws are changing and society is taking this problem more seriously. Victims of both rape and sexual harassment feel robbed of their self-respect and of control over their own body. The media have failed to show how sex crimes really hurt individual victims, their families, and all of society.

CRITICAL THINKING
A woman met a man and, a few days later, agreed to have sex with him. She requested that he use protection. Yet, he was strong and powerful and, at the last minute, tore off the condom he was wearing. He knew he was HIV-positive. The woman became infected. The court found him guilty of criminal negligence. The judge said that the woman was partly to blame because a reasonable person would not be so quick to have sex. What is your opinion?

Understanding Chapter 15

1. What is sexual assault, and who can be sexually assaulted?
2. How is a rape trial different from all other criminal trials?
3. What is sexual harassment?

 Workbook
Self-Check p.32
Reality-Check p.33

☞ **TO LEARN MORE**
Government Today, p. 97

Chapter 16

When a Family Becomes Violent

Jim B. was an engineer. He and his wife had three children. Jim and his wife started abusing drugs. Pretty soon, they would use drugs every night after work. When the children returned from school, if they did not do their chores or homework properly, they would receive a beating. The drug abuse got worse and so did the beatings. Jim and his wife lost complete control of their behavior when abusing drugs. One night, Jim hurt his youngest daughter so badly that she died. He had thrown her against a wall. She died from an injury to the head.

CHECK vocabulary words in bold. LOOK UP word meanings in the glossary beginning on page 92.

CRITICAL THINKING
What do you think is the difference between punishment that is OK and a beating that is not OK?

Social worker Judy Z. says: "My family was attacked. One sister was raped and another seriously hurt. Yet, because our family is so close, I could get past the violence that had made us victims. I always felt safe. Young people need to learn how to raise a family. Most teen parents do not have family life skills. They also teach violence at home without even knowing it. If a person grows up feeling unsafe, he or she grows up not needing to feel safe. He or she learns to live in danger. That is sad."

Jim B. was found guilty of murder. Neighbors were shocked because, to outsiders in the community, the family had always seemed to be perfectly normal. But a family that abuses drugs is never normal. It is also often violent. In this chapter, you will learn what the law says about family violence. It can happen in every kind of family, rich or poor. You will learn what help the law gives to victims of family violence.

Family Violence Law

The law used to say that a wife and children were like property that belonged to the husband or father. The father could do whatever he wanted and was the boss. Women and children had very few rights.

Today, things are different. Many states have family courts to deal with family problems. There are now laws that treat all members of a family fairly. It is illegal for anyone to be **abused**, or hurt. **Spouse abuse** occurs when a spouse is hurt by a partner. When children are hurt, we have cases of **child abuse**. The hurt can be physical or emotional.

Child Abuse and Child Neglect

What is child abuse? Child abuse means harming a child's mind or body. For example, Steve R. became very angry when he heard his four-year-old son, Tim, cry. Steve would hit him to make him stop. One day he hit Tim too hard and broke his arm. Steve's wife, Jane, took their son to the hospital. Tim was crying and extremely upset emotionally.

When the doctor asked how Tim had broken his arm, Jane said that Tim had fallen in the playground. The doctor did not believe the story. He could tell the difference between a broken bone from falling and a broken bone from a beating.

The law says that the doctor must report suspected child abuse. Tim's doctor called **child protection** services. People from the services came to talk to Tim's parents. They wanted to work with them to make their home safe for Tim so he could return home. But first, Tim went to stay in a **foster** home for a while.

Sometimes, child abuse is not reported. Neighbors do not like to become involved. The child may be too young, afraid, or ashamed to tell anyone. One parent may not want to report the other parent who did the hurting. The abusing parent usually is too ashamed to tell anyone.

In the case of Jim B. and his family, although the parents were highly respected in the community, one teacher did remember seeing bruises on two of the children's faces a couple of times. The children would make excuses. They were too afraid to tell the truth.

At first, when the death of Jim B.'s daughter was discovered, nobody could believe that it. Child abuse and family violence can happen in any family. It does not matter where the family lives or how much money the family has.

How can you report child abuse? An abused child can tell an adult whom he or she trusts. This adult might be a teacher, a religious leader, or parent of a friend. The adult should then call the **child welfare agency** for the child. Most states have a hotline for reporting child abuse.

Will the abuser know who reported the abuse? The answer is no. This information is kept secret. A child-welfare worker will visit the family to find out what is happening. This person's job will be to decide how the family's problems can be solved.

The law says that friends and neighbors do not have to report suspected child abuse. By contrast, teachers, doctors, and social workers must report what they suspect is happening.

If a person lives with someone who is abusing a child, the law says that the person who knows but does nothing to try to stop it might also be guilty of child abuse. Often, women are afraid to stop the abuse of another family member because they are also being abused.

Child Neglect: Is child neglect the same as child abuse? The answer is no. **Neglect** means not taking good enough care of a child so that the child physical or mental health is harmed. Parents might leave a small child alone and uncared for. Children who are left alone might play with matches and cause a deadly fire that kills innocent people.

Some parents do not feed or clothe a child properly. For example, when the police came to Jim B.'s house, they found that the other children had not been well cared for. They were very hungry, their clothing was torn, and they had not had a bath for days. The children had been neglected. It does not take abuse to harm the health of a child.

People who suspect child neglect should call the child welfare agency or social services department right away. It might save a child's life. Parents who neglect or abuse their children need help. Often, such parents know they are doing something wrong. By talking to them, they might be convinced to seek help on their own. Yet, they may be afraid they will be arrested and their children taken from them.

What happens after suspected child abuse has been reported? A social worker investigates, or carefully checks out, the case. Then the child welfare agency decides what to do. It may put the child in a foster home, which could be the home of a relative or a foster parent.

What are foster parents? Usually, they are good people who like caring for children. Often, their own children have already grown up and left home. Foster parents apply for a license from the state. But first, child-welfare workers visit them to make sure they are responsible. They check that the home is safe and clean.

Do parents who are guilty of abuse go to court? The child welfare agency helps the parents get help. Sometimes, they go to court. This happens if the injuries are serious or if the abuse has gone on for a long time.

Most cases are handled in family court. The courts may punish the parents by sending them to jail. The court will usually order help for the family in trying to keep it together. Its main goal is to do what is best for the child.

What if someone reports child abuse by mistake? Sometimes, abuse is reported when abuse has not taken place. Most states have computers to keep records of abuse cases. Even if a suspected child abuser is reported but never arrested or convicted, his or her name could be in the computer. This can be like an arrest record. For example, if someday the reported abuser wanted to work in a day-care center or as a foster parent, this name would be listed as a suspected child abuser. He or she would not get the job.

Can a name ever be taken out of the computer? If a suspect is not guilty of child abuse, the name can be cleared from the computer. Talking to the agency that handled the abuse case can help. Find out about the laws in your state.

What is sexual abuse of children? **Sexual abuse** happens when another person uses a child for sexual reasons. This is similar to rape and sexual harassment that you have already learned about. **Incest** is committed when members of a family have sex with each other. Both sexual abuse and incest are against the law and very, very wrong. Everyone in the family is hurt by them.

In most cases of sexual abuse of children, the abuser is someone close to the child. Most cases involve an adult and a child.

Sexual abuse happens more often than the reports show. Families try to keep quiet about it. The children become afraid and ashamed.

A sexually abused child should tell an adult whom he or she trusts.

The People's Publishing Group, Inc.: *Crime and the Law*

The adult should report the crime to the child welfare agency that handles such cases. It then might go to family court. Some serious cases are sent to criminal court. They might be treated as rape cases.

CRITICAL THINKING
Can a person both love and hate another person at the same time? Why do you think this way?

Spouse Abuse

What is spouse abuse? Spouse abuse means beating a husband or a wife. It also means beating your boyfriend or girlfriend. Most of the time, spouse abuse involves a man beating the woman with whom he lives or with whom he has a close relationship. An abused spouse is also called a battered spouse.

What can a battered spouse do? Battered, or beaten, spouses are frightened that their partners will do them further harm if they tell. They do not know where to go to be safe. They sometimes do not know how to get enough money to take care of their children if they should leave. Spouse-beating is not a private family matter. It is a crime.

It is also a crime that can turn into murder. Either the man can kill the woman, or the woman can kill the man because they cannot think of another way to help themselves. Yet, there are several ways to stop the abuse from building into a loss of life. Nobody ever needs to a life because of abuse.

A spouse can get help from a center or shelter. A shelter is a place where one can take one's children or just oneself for safety. A person can stay there while making plans to live far away from the abuser.

A woman can file charges against her husband or boyfriend. She can get an **injunction** or order of protection against him. This means that he would not be allowed to come near her. If he does, she could have him arrested. A man can protect himself against a wife or a girlfriend in the same way.

DID YOU KNOW? Abuse can be passed on in families from generation to generation as "normal" behavior. But abuse is *never* normal.

When should a spouse go to the police? A spouse should go to the police station to file charges as soon as possible after the first beating or threat of a beating. The victim must make sure that the police keep a record of any injuries received. This can be later be used as evidence in court.

Even after the abuse, some spouses still want to live with their partners. They might love them and keep hoping that the abuser will change behavior. The truth is that people who abuse people they love do not change unless they get help. The family court can make sure this happens.

What can a victim do during a beating? The victim can call the police. The police may not arrest the abuser if they do not actually see the attack. Yet, if the suspect has a weapon, the suspect can be arrested.

If the police do not arrest the abuser, the victim should ask the police to stay while getting some clothes and whatever else is needed to go somewhere else. She should then get out of the house.

What happens after an arrest or complaint? There are many different things that can happen. Some cases might go to family court. Some cases might go to criminal or district court. Some cases are

EYE OPENER Between 1976 and 1987, one out of three murdered women was killed by her husband.

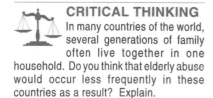
dropped. If the courts offer counseling for couples, only sometimes does it stop the abuse.

What if you witness a beating? If you see or hear a beating while it is going on, call the police. The police will not tell who called them. If you know that these attacks happen often, you may try to talk to the person being abused.

In talking to the abused, do not ask a lot of questions. Be friendly. Give the abused person time to talk about the problem. The victim will gradually trust you as a good listener. If the person then decides to take action, go with the victim to court, and testify as a witness.

All people who are abused could be in constant danger. Victim-assistance programs can help victims to find safety and to even start a brand new life.

What is elderly abuse? **Elderly abuse** is the abuse of older people or senior citizens. About 5 percent of older people in the United States are abused. Many states have laws that give more punishment for elderly abuse than for other types of assault. This is because elderly people really cannot defend themselves.

For example, Tina's grandmother lives with her. The grandmother is very old. She cannot take care of herself. She does not always get to the bathroom in time. She makes messes. Tina hates to clean up after her. Sometimes, Tina gets so mad that she hits her grandmother. She knows it is wrong, but she cannot stop herself. Tina is guilty of elderly abuse. Do you know anyone like Tina?

What be done about elderly abuse? Elderly abuse can be reported to the Office of Aging or to the police. The family can get help with counseling. The elderly person might be put in a hospital or nursing home in order to be safe. Stopping violence in the home can benefit the whole community. The end of family violence can lead to a truly peaceful society.

 Workbook
Self-Check p.34
Reality-Check p.35

 TO LEARN MORE
Drug Education, p. 93

Understanding Chapter 16

1. What is child abuse?
2. What is an injunction?
3. What help is there for violent families

IN THIS PART, YOU WILL LEARN

■analyze what is positive and negative about gangs ■discover what gang life is really about ■weight the importance of your own values again the risks and dangers of gang life ■advise a younger person or peer wisely about whether or not to join a gang ■make decisions about issues in your life that are not represented truthfully in the media

Making Decisions

COOPERATIVE LEARNING ACTIVITY

Running with the wrong crowd

Sometimes, young people say that it is unrealistic to try to avoid violence and gangs. Often, what they mean is either that peer pressure or their pride might be involved or that they do no believe that nonviolent alternatives really work. They often find themselves wanting something to belong to. But gangs not only abuse society; they also abuse their own members, and there is no pride in that. Explore with your small group the truth about what gangs have to offer.

Scene: John and Tanya were members of the Four-X gang. They had dated for years and planned to marry. Gang life seemed exciting. Both John and Tanya had no family and were very loyal to each other. They loved each other. Then one day, there was a big drug deal. Several members were involved, including John and Tanya. The police came and there was a shootout. John got desperate and hid behind a car. Putting his arm around Tanya's neck, he pointed his gun to her head. "Stop or I'll shoot!" he screamed to the police. Tanya could not believe her ears.

Can a "friend" who has no respect for society really be a friend to you?

1. Read over the scene above. In your small group, develop a two-minute role play. Discuss the role-play, focusing on what your group has discovered about gangs and gang loyalty in this scene.

2. Brainstorm everything your group thinks it knows about gangs. Have one person write down the information. List at least ten items. Write each item in a square on a piece of cardboard. Cut out the individual squares and sort them into two piles—one being the plus group and the other being the minus. The plus group should have items that some people thought were good reasons to join a gang. The minus group should have items that some people thought were reasons to stay away from gangs.

3. Weigh the plus items altogether in a scale. Then weigh just the minus items. (Or weigh both piles in a two-sided scale like the scales of justice). Which pile has the greater weight? By how much?

4. Brainstorm a list of other kinds of groups or activities that can satisfy some of the positives that have nothing to do with abuse or criminal gang behavior. For example, if a plus item was a "feeling of belonging," an item on your group's list might be "finding a big sister or big brother organization in your community."

While reading this chapter...

Stop and think about how important your values are to you, such as whether or not you could be forced to do something against your will.

Chapter 17

Stopping Crime Where You Live

Drug dealers were using an empty apartment building near a highway. Drug users would drive into this area to buy drugs and drive away. For three years, the police kept arresting the dealers. Drugs always bring serious crime to a community. There were many murders in the area and so many calls for help that the police did not have enough officers to send. Finally, the people in the community formed an action group.

CHECK vocabulary words in bold. LOOK UP word meanings in the glossary beginning on page 92.

They called a meeting of the police, city government officials, community leaders, the health department, the public works department, the housing department, and lawyers. Together, this group came up with a plan to rid the neighborhood of drugs and drug dealers. The plan was successful, and the neighborhood became a safe one for families. In this chapter, you will learn about the causes of crime. You will also learn about the many ways citizens and police can work together as a team to stop crime.

Citizen Patrols

The police departments of some major cities have neighborhood people who patrol and guard their area against crime. They are called citizen foot patrols. They are police trained, carry phones, and wear special jackets. They can call the police if they see trouble but, often, do not carry guns.

How much have citizen patrols helped? Property crimes have dropped by 44 percent in Portland, Oregon, where there is an active foot patrol. This means that people are stealing less because they know they have a good chance of getting caught. Also, not one single person has been hurt while on patrol in Portland!

The Causes of Crime

Many people believe that **poverty** and unemployment cause many crimes. People who do not have money often live in crowded places where rent is lower. People living in crowded places get in each other's way. They argue and fight more, so there is more chance for violence.

CRITICAL THINKING
What do you think is the cause of crime? Do you think there is more than one cause? Explain.

Former gang member Pedro says: "I heard fellow gang members say they expect to be killed with all the shooting they do. It is true: the only direction a gang takes you in is toward jail or toward the cemetery. That's because gangs set out to abuse society, and that is a loser. I was beating up on other black and Puerto Rican kids when I should have been working with them to fight prejudice. It is just plain wrong to hurt other human beings, no matter what their color is."

The People's Publishing Group, Inc.: *Crime and the Law*

For example, when the number of jobs goes down, the murder rate goes up. This is also because people who do not have jobs have more time to get in trouble. They may then start to sell drugs or steal to get money to live. It is easy for the crimes they commit to become more and more serious. The sad mistake many people make is that they do not make other choices to change their unhappy situation.

Sometimes, people who have lots of money commit crimes. For example, white-collar criminals can steal very large amounts of money from businesses.

Many people believe that violence on TV, in the movies, and in rock music helps cause crime. They are right. If people see and hear so much violence, they will begin to think that violence is the way to handle problems. Of course, violence is never the way to solve problems. This is the most important message that people do not learn from the media. Violence may seem normal on TV, but violence is never normal.

Society has changed. Families do not always teach young people about what is right and what is wrong. Many families have a hard time living on little money. There may be only one parent to take care of everybody's needs, or the parents may be young. Teen parents often are not able to get a good job or to make wise decisions about life. They also have a hard time being responsible.

Such families can have a lot of violence. Problems do not get solved and anger builds. Society needs to help these families by working together. Programs that provide jobs and counseling help make families stronger. Strong families mean less crime.

Working Together

How can working together stop crime? Many young people get in trouble because they are bored and have nothing to do after school. They may also get in trouble because they are not in school during the day. Being both unhappy and bored is a dangerous mix.

When one community found that many of its young people had been suspended from school, it started a special program for these dropouts. As a result, the daytime or schooltime burglary rate went down. Many cities have after-school programs with activities to keep young people busy, interested in projects, and off the street. If young people are off the street, they do not have to spend time with those who are a bad influence and who will get them into trouble.

Mediation

How can crime among people who know each other be stopped? Many crimes are committed by people who know each other. Often, the victim may not want to bring charges against the suspect. The victim may think that the suspect should have another chance. The victim may be afraid of the suspect. This is where **mediation** can help.

What is mediation? The victim brings charges. If the victim brings charges in court, the court decides whether or not the case is one that can

The People's Publishing Group, Inc.: *Crime and the Law*

CRITICAL THINKING
Most gang members come from families and neighborhoods where money is scarce. Yet, most people who are unhappy or who do not have much money never become involved in crime. What are some of the ways to create a better life within the law in today's world?

DID YOU KNOW? For thousands of years, Mohawk Indians have used mediation even for crimes of murder. Three things are important in Mohawk mediation: 1) the defendant has to understand what is wrong and agree to change; 2) both sides have to agree at the ideas talked about to solve the situation are OK; and 3) the defendant has to do something to make up for the harm caused the victim or the loss of the family and friends of the victim.

EYE OPENER Youth gangs have become an all-too-common part of city life, from Los Angeles to New York. In Los Angeles, gangs have more than 70,000 members in 600 gangs. This is according to Keith E. Greenberg in his book, *Out of the Gang*.

be solved by mediation. If the victim knows a mediation center, she can go to it. At the mediation center, there are people called mediators. Their job is to listen to both sides of the argument. The mediator tries to "sew up" the tear in the community that results from the anger about the crime that has torn it apart.

Here is an example of a situation that was solved outside of court. Rosie M. liked to listen to very loud music. Her neighbor, Kathy, worked at night and had to sleep during the day. Kathy had often asked Rosie to turn down the music. Rosie would do this for a day or two, but then forget and turn it back up.

Rosie and Kathy started to argue. Kathy was so upset that she damaged Rosie's tape player. Rosie decided to go to a mediation center. The mediator listened to both sides. They agreed that Kathy would buy Rosie another tape deck to pay back her loss. They also agreed that Rosie would buy earphones to use during the hours that Kathy needs quiet. This would pay Kathy back for the sleep she had lost.

The problem has worked out between the two people without the need and cost of a court. Programs like these do not have due-process rules. This is because most of them do not deal with serious felonies. But the results are still fair, and everyone is happy with them. The crime that took place stopped happening.

When the crimes people report happen to be felonies, mediation programs take care of these crimes more quickly than courts. They also do not cost the suspect any money. Of course, really serious crimes *must* be handled by the courts.

The Community

How can community groups stop crime? A community is a large group of people living in one area. People working in a community can stop crime. For example, there are the citizen patrols and auxiliary police who watch out for crimes. There is also a neighborhood watch program. This means that all the people in the neighborhood watch for crimes. People might see from their windows criminal activity down in the street. If they see something happening, they call the police.

Community Policing

What is community policing? These days, people are talking a lot about community policing. Here, the police work with the community in a way that respects the problems and the rights of every individual as well as of the community as a whole. This includes building a greater understanding between the people and the police—building a partnership. The police cannot do everything that is needed to prevent crime and build a safe society by themselves.

Think back to the start of this chapter to the example of the successful plan to rid a neighborhood of drug dealers. The following are the steps in that plan:

1. Stop the buying and selling of drugs. Most of the users were people

from the suburbs on their way home from work. The community group felt sure that these buyers would fear losing their job or going to jail.

2. Put up signs saying that the police will arrest all drug buyers in the area. People who lived in the area got stickers to put on their cars that gave the same warning. Others who came into the neighborhood were questioned politely by the police.

3. Have the lawyers find out who owns the empty buildings. The lawyers can then have the owners either make their buildings safe or tear them down. Many owners chose to tear down their buildings, so the drug dealers had no place to hide!

As a result of these three steps, very few drug buyers came into the area. Drug selling was greatly reduced, and the police did not have to make many arrests. The community group's plan helps to keep crime down both in the present and in the future.

The police and the community also cleaned up the area. In one day, ten trailer-sized garbage trucks of dirt and garbage were filled.

How did the community win in this situation? Calls for police help went down by 44 percent. This means that crime went down by one third. Also, people got to know the police better and vice verso. A sense of trust in the community had been achieved.

Today, many police departments are trying to recruit more people from neighborhoods to become police officers. They believe that if there are more police officer of both sexes and from all backgrounds. There will be more trust between the police and the communities they serve.

What else can communities do? Every summer, there is a special night all across the country called, "America's National Night Out." On this night, everyone's job is to watch out for crime. Your local police station has information on how you can help next year. Of course, watching out for crime to help stop crime even before it happens is what everyone should do each day of the year.

Mediation Programs

What can schools do to prevent crime? Many schools have antiviolence programs and mediation programs. These programs help students learn work out problems between each other before they become serious or physically violent.

For example, a student named Tara had a boyfriend who started to date another girl. Tara heard that they were saying mean things about her. She became angry and made the mistake of bringing a knife to school. She was ready to hurt the other girl. However, the school had a mediation program.

Mediators persuaded Tara and the other girl to agree to mediation. By talking to the other girl, Tara found out that the girl had not said mean things about her. Tara calmed down and nobody was hurt. Violence had been successfully prevented.

Where do mediation programs start? They can start in elementary school. Many schools in New York City work with a program

CRITICAL THINKING How can better day-care, parent training, and other social services help a community to reduce crime?

DID YOU KNOW? In the future, the president is plan-ning to create areas in communities called empowerment zones. To empower means to give strength. The people, working together in these zones, would help young people find something to say yes to that is good for their lives, while helping them say no to drugs, crime, and violence.

EYE OPENER One-third of gang-violence victims are innocent bystanders.

CRITICAL THINKING
There is a strong movement in the United States to refuse three-time offenders parole or subsequent freedom because they do not seem to have been rehabilitated. Do you think this a good idea?

called *The Resolving Conflict Creatively Program*. This means solving arguments by thinking carefully and talking about problems. The program teaches everyone how to stop violence before it happens. Even kindergarten students can learn how to using talking to prevent fighting.

The problem of gangs or groups of young people committing crimes as a group is growing all across America. The great amount of crime that people always thought was only in big cities has spread to small cities, towns, and even farm areas. Gangs also fight with each other and cause much violence.

Schools can also plan activities that keep students busy, safe, and away from gangs. Many people belong to gangs partly because they like to do things with friends in a group. But young people can always be part of a school group.

Schools can also talk with parents about how to stop illegal gang activity. For example, there might be late-night sports programs run by people who are also trained in mediation. Of course, such a program only works if all parents attend, and especially the parents of students who are in danger of getting into trouble.

How can first offenders be stopped from becoming second offenders? Committing a crime once is a mistake. Committing a crime a second time is a serious mistake. Many people believe that preventing crime also means preventing first offenders from committing more crimes.

When inmates come out of prison after their first offense, if they cannot find jobs and they are still unhappy, they might commit more crimes. That is the time when people need to make the right choices. This can repeat over and over again until their not making the right choice becomes like a snowball rolling down a mountain.

DID YOU KNOW? Many of Eleanor M.'s family members were killed by people with guns. To fight back, she formed a group called Mothers and Men Against Gangs. The group sets a curfew for the neighborhood and gets gang members to do community work. In Eleanor M.'s neighborhood in Los Angeles, California, because of her work with gangs, drive-by shootings (shootings by criminals in moving vehicles) have been greatly reduced.

Education is the Key

In New York, a program was started by young prisoners to fellow inmates to become educated while in prison. The program teaches inmates the skills needed to get and keep a job.

This program helps inmates be better able to get along by doing the right thing outside of prison. Inmates also know that more education means a better chance of getting a job, even in hard times. They discover that education is the key to staying out of jail.

Workbook
Self-Check p.36
Reality-Check p.37

☞ **TO LEARN MORE**
The Peoples Guide to:
Drug Education, pp. 8-10, 98-99

Understanding Chapter 17

1. What are some of the causes of crime?
2. Describe what you know about community policing.
3. Explain how people can solve the legal problems of a crime out of court.

Chapter 18

Safe Streets and Homes

Greg D. liked to hang out with Willie because Willie was tough. He made Greg feel safe in the streets. One day, Willie said to Greg and his friends, "Let's go bother some people in the subway." Greg was too afraid to say no. "We're not going to hurt anybody, are we?" Greg asked. "No, we'll just harass them," said Willie. They went into the subway.

Willie approached some people on the platform to rob them while the others waited. Suddenly, he turned around, a knife in his hand and blood all over him. One of the victims had fought back and been stabbed to death. "Run!" Willie shouted. They ran, but the police caught them.

Greg was frightened even though he knew that he had done nothing wrong. The police told him his *Miranda* rights — that he had the right to remain silent. Greg thought he would just tell them what happened and not be in trouble. The police videotaped everyone as evidence. Today, they are all in prison, serving a twenty-five-years-to-life sentence for a murder they had never even planned to commit.

In this chapter, you will learn about saving your life by staying far away from trouble. You will learn how young people all over the country are stopping violence and crime in ways that can really work.

CHECK vocabulary words in bold. LOOK UP word meanings in the glossary beginning on page 92.

CRITICAL THINKING
Can you think of people you admire who are nonviolent? How do they deal with anger and conflict?

Say No to Crime

Can you say no to crime? Small crimes have a way of turning into big crimes. Willie probably did not plan to kill anyone. He knew he only wanted to rob some people. But he had a knife, and he picked a woman who looked as if she would not struggle. He was wrong. As a result, a knife plus a plan had equaled murder.

What could Greg have done to stop this crime? Could Greg have said no to tagging along? Could he have said he wanted to do something else? Should Greg have been a better boss of himself? You alone are the boss of your own behavior-nobody else!

Friends

It is easier to say no to a small crime before it turns into something big than to stop a big crime. Sometimes, you might need help saying no. You may be afraid that your friends will hurt you or think you are not

Street kid Gino says: "I used to belong to a gang. I thought they were my best friends. All I got for my loyalty was trouble. Friends like that plus alcohol, drugs, or weapons equals murder. Think about it."

"cool" if you do not go along with them. They may even call you names and try to make you angry.

When this happens, is there one adult you trust who can help you say no? Are you strong enough, smart enough, and cool enough to stand up to your friends? You can say that you have things to do at home. You can have another idea of a fun thing to do that does not hurt anybody. You have a right to say no.

Sometimes, people—especially young people—get into trouble just by being with people who are doing criminal things. Sometimes, they do not even agree to commit a crime before it happens. Sometimes, they are bystanders who are taken by surprise. Look at the case of Dina G.

Tricked into Crime

Dina G. liked going out with Reggie. He always had lots of money and bought her nice clothes and jewelry. But she did not know that he was a drug dealer.

One weekend, he invited her to go on a trip to Washington. He had secretly planned to pick up some drugs from a drug seller. Dina and Reggie drove in his car to the pickup place. Dina still had no idea what was happening. What Reggie did not know was that the police were watching him.

After Reggie picked up the drugs, he told Dina he had decided to stay in Washington alone for a couple of days. He gave Inez the car and asked her to drive it back to New York. The police waited until she had crossed the state line from Delaware into New Jersey. Reggie's illegal act had just now become a federal offense because something illegal had been transported from one state into another.

Dina was arrested. There was a kilogram, or about a pound, of an illegal drug in the trunk of the car. Although shocked and an innocent victim, Dina was charged with possession and with crossing a state line with drugs. The judge set bail at $1.5 million.

Could what happened to Dina ever happen to you? If you made a list of your friends, which ones would you most likely hangout with? Why? What things do you like to do together? Could any of these activities turn into trouble? What can you do to so that this never happens to you?

You Have the Power to Stop Violence: Do you know someone who has been killed? Was that person killed by someone he knew? Half of the homicides in the United States happen between people who know each other. Often, the people are even in the same family!

People do not start out planning to murder their brother, cousin, sister, or friend. They argue. The fight gets out of control. Sometimes, there are weapons around. Someone grabs a gun or a knife. Sometimes, one person may go away and then return with friends or come back with a gun or a knife. Half of the time, at least one person in the fight has been drinking or taking drugs. A person under the influence of a substance that causes them to lose control of their behavior is dangerous.

The People's Publishing Group, Inc.: *Crime and the Law*

The police say that if there were not so many guns and knives around, there would not be so many murders. Why is this so? It is hard to kill someone with your fists. Unfortunately, it is all too easy to kill someone with a gun or a knife.

The police say that if people did not drink so much there would be fewer murders. Why is this? It is because when people drink they lose control of their behavior. They cannot think clearly. They do things they would not do if they were not drunk. That is why alcohol, like a gun, can be a kind of weapon.

Many community groups are trying to control guns and drinking by helping people understand the problems that they cause. The police say that they have a hard time doing anything about the violence between people who know each other. That is why the community needs to help. Police cannot break up every fight that happens in someone's kitchen or living room.

You can keep yourself from getting into fights. This will not stop all of the family violence in your community, but it could keep you from being hurt or even murdered someday. It could also keep you from hurting somebody else. It could keep you out of prison.

Why should you stop fighting? Many people think that not fighting means you are frightened. There are times when you may have to fight to defend or protect yourself—to keep safe. However, most of the time, you do not need to fight. It probably takes more courage not to fight than to fight. Think about it!

Because so many people have the wrong idea that fighting is the only way or the best way to solve problems, they make fun of those who do not fight. These people are wrong. These people are not smart.

If you think about friends you know who have been badly hurt in fights, what were the fights about? Would you have given up your life for those reasons? Can you imagine going to prison for those reasons? After all, almost everyone who acts in a violent way toward someone they know gets caught and punished.

Many fights start out small and become more serious. They escalate. Violence becomes possible. Then, in a while, the murder can happen.

Kevin S. and his friend Tyrone had been arrested two years before for robbing another student. Tyrone thought information Kevin had given the police about the past crime had gotten Tyrone convicted. Tyrone had been angry with Kevin ever since and had threatened Kevin several times. Kevin said that he believed he had to kill Tyrone in order to protect himself. Kevin shot him in the hallway of their high school.

The jury believed that Kevin was very frightened. There was evidence that he was about to change his mind when the gun went off. He was convicted of manslaughter instead of murder and must now serve many years in prison. At the trial, the mother of the victim screamed, "Somebody has to get him—he killed my son!" She was very angry at the jury for only convicting him of manslaughter when her son was dead.

The People's Publishing Group, Inc.: *Crime and the Law*

CRITICAL THINKING
Why is it that talking through conflict can leave both people satisfied, but that using violence leaves nobody satisfied? How can role-play help to solve conflict?

DID YOU KNOW? There are certain ages when young people are much more at risk of being involved in criminal activity, partly because of peer pressure.

EYE OPENER According to the Uniform Crime Reports for the U.S., the total number of arrests for fourteen-year-olds was more than 500,000, while the number for fifteen-year-olds dropped to 270,000. For sixteen-year-olds, it rose to 326,000 and continued to rise until age nineteen. After that, numbers again began to fall.

Do you think this trial was really the end of a crime that started two years ago—when two friends decided to commit a robbery? Do you think anyone else connected to these two young men might get hurt in the future?

How can you stop fighting? Cool down and calm down. Arguing often builds into fighting and violence. Less fighting means less crime. Here are some things that you can do to stop fighting. People who are trained in **martial arts** like judo or tae kwon do say that these steps really work! Practice them for yourself — especially when you almost in a fight situation.

1. Take a deep breath. Relax before you say anything. Speak softly and slowly in low tones.

2. Keep your body relaxed. Check that your hands are not in a tight fist. Make sure you do not look as if you will hit someone.

3. Decide to let go of the anger. It's not worth it. Think of your anger as a package. Throw the package away. Some people will start a fight if someone just steps on their sneakers, pushes against them in the hallway, or says something nasty. What if somebody says something nasty about your mother? Doesn't she want you alive and in school? If you fight and get hurt or suspended from school, will she be happy? Think about it.

4. Do something that is not expected. This means that the other person will expect you to do one thing, so do another. The person may expect you to be ready to fight or to be very frightened. If you are friendly and relaxed, it will confuse the person. There will probably be no fight as a result.

Can you think of a way to let the other person leave without feeling like a coward? The other person might be worried about how he looks to friends. What if you just apologized or said, "Excuse me"? It would not mean that you were wrong and the other person was right. It would just mean that you understood that the person was upset. Try it.

5. Listen to what the other person is saying. Really try to understand what the person is saying. Many times we do not really listen to other people. We are too busy thinking of what we will say or do next. Practice listening with your friends and with your enemies. Tell yourself that you can find a solution to the problem. Also, convince the other person that you can find a solution to it.

How can you make your school safer? Many schools have mediation programs. You learned about some of them in Chapter 17. What do mediators do? They listen to each person in the argument tell their story. But there are rules for talking. The rules are these:

1. No name calling

2. No cursing or swearing

3. Only one person can talk at a time, while the other person listens

After everyone has listened to everyone else, they agree on what to do next. For example, a high school boy threw a piece of chalk at a girl. She

The People's Publishing Group, Inc.: *Crime and the Law*

called him names. He called her names. They threatened each other. At lunchtime, she started to call members of her gang. People talked about weapons and violence.

The principal called the boy and the girl into her office and gave them a choice. They could let a mediator work with them, or they could be suspended. They agreed to mediate with a sixteen-year-old classmate. It took an hour to talk about how angry they both were. At the end, they signed a contract to stop fighting and to tell their gangs to go home.

"Mediation has cut our suspension rate in half," says the school principal. If your school has a mediation program, find out more about it. Mediation is for everybody. If your school does not have a mediation program, find out what programs there are in your city. Find out if your school can become part of one. Mediation works!

How can you stop your friends from getting hurt? Many times, people let a fight grow because they do not want to look weak in front of their friends. But you can help your friends by helping to cool things down. Letting them know that you do not think it is weak to walk away; It is smart and strong.

For example, a friend is angry because of something someone says. He wants you to come along to find that person. You can say, "It's not worth it. Let's go play ball." You could be saving someone's life. You do this by being nonviolent.

CRITICAL THINKING
Fights do not just happen. Certain steps lead up to them. What are some of these steps? Think about the role of emotions, peer pressure, and signs of trouble that do not involve words.

DID YOU KNOW? Gang activity, and all of the violence and drug crimes that are part of it, is spreading like wildfire from large cities to small towns and farm areas. This is the happening because of gang networks or systems that have been set up over large areas by member gangs.

Understanding Chapter 18
1. Why is it important to know how to keep fights from becoming serious?
2. What are three things you can do to cool things down?
3. What are the rules for mediation?

 Workbook
Self-Check p.38
Reality-Check p.39

☛ **TO LEARN MORE**
The Peoples Guide to:
Drug Education, pp. 3-5, 12-19, 33-36, 90-92

GLOSSARY

English	Definition	Spanish
Abuse (uh-BYOOS)	Mistreatment of a sexual, physical, or emotional nature; battering; beating; hurting.	Maltrato de una naturaleza sexual, física o emocional. Una golpiza o agresión. Hacer daño.
Academy (uh-CAH-duh-mee)	A school for training.	Escuela de entrenamiento.
Acquit (uh-KWIT)	To find not guilty.	No hallar culpabilidad.
Adversary (AD-vur-seh-ree) in court	One who is against another.	Una persona en contra de otra.
Age of consent (kun-SENT)	The age when the law says a person may agree to a sexual act.	Edad a la cual la ley dice que una persona puede acceder a un acto sexual.
Amendment (uh-MEND-ment)	A change or an addition that makes something better; the first ten amendments to the U.S. Constitution are known as the Bill of Rights.	Un cambio o adición que hace algo mejor. Las primeras diez enmiendas de la Constitución de los E.E.U.U. se conocen como la Carta de Derechos.
Appeal (uh-PEEL)	To bring a case to a higher court for review of the decision.	Traer un caso a una corte mas alta para revisar la decisión.
Appellate court (uh-PEH-lit)	A court that hears appeals; also called a court of appeals.	Una corte donde se oyen apelaciones. También es llamada corte de apelaciones.
Arraignment (uh-RAYN-ment)	The first appearance in court after arrest.	La primera aparición ante la corte después del arresto.
Arrest (uh-REST)	To hold a person in custody because the person has been charged to answer for a crime	Mantener una persona bajo custodia porque a esa persona se le ha ordenado que responda por un delito.
Arrest warrant (uh-REST WAR-rent)	A court order that gives the police the right to take a person into custody.	Una órden de la corte que le da a la policía el derecho de arrestar a una persona.
Arson (AR-sun)	Setting fire to another person's property.	Darle fuego a la propiedad ajena.
Assault (uh-SAWLT)	A threat or an attempt to injure another person physically.	Una amenaza o intento de agredir a otra persona físicamente.
Bail	Money or property that you give to the court as proof that you will show for the trial.	Dinero o propiedad que se da a la corte como prueba de que usted comparecerá para el juicio.
Bar association (ah-soh-see-AY-shun)	An organization to which all qualified lawyers belong.	Organización a la cual pertenecen todos los abogados calificados.
Battery (BA-tuh-ree)	Unlawful or illegal physical contact with another person when this other person does not agree with it.	Contacto físico ilícito o ilegal con una persona que no está de acuerdo con ello.
Behavior (bee-HAYV-yur)	The way a person acts; what a person says and does.	La forma en que actúa una persona o lo que ésta dice y hace.
Bias crime (By-is)	A crime committed against someone by a person who is against the victim for no good reason.	Un crimen que se comete contra alguien por una persona que está en su contra sin una buena razón.
Book	When the police arrest a person who is under suspicion, they take a picture and fingerprint the subject and record the suspect's name, age, and address.	Cuando la policía arresta a una persona sospechosa y se le toma una fotografía, las huellas digitales y se asienta su nombre, edad y dirección en el informe.

GLOSSARY

Border (BAWR-dur)	The place where one country's or state's land stops and another country or state begins.	El lugar donde termina un país o estado y donde comienza otro país o estado.
Burglary (BUR-gluh-ree)	Breaking into a building in order to commit a crime.	Entrar a un edificio para cometer un delito.
Bystander (BY-stan-dur)	A person who is at an event but does not take part in it.	Una persona presente en un evento pero sin embargo no participa en el.
Cell	A small, almost empty room with bars where a prisoner is kept locked up.	Una habitación con barrotes, pequeña y casi vacía donde se mantiene encerrados a los prisioneros.
Character witness (KAH-rak-tur WIT-nes)	Someone who testifies that the suspect has a good character; this witness could be a teacher, employer, or minister.	Alguien cuyo testimonio indica que un sospechoso tiene buena conducta. Este testigo puede ser un maestro, patrón o ministro.
Charge	An explanation of all the elements that are involved in the legal accusation of a crime.	La explicación detodos los elementos involucrados en la acusación legal de un delito.
Child welfare agency (WEL-fayr-AY-jen-cee)	The government office that looks after the health or well-being of children.	La agencia gubernamental que ve por la salud y el bienestar de los niños.
Citizen's arrest (SIH-tih-zenz uh-REST)	An arrest made by someone who is not a police officer.	An arresto llevado a cabo por alguien que no es un agente de la policía.
Civil (SIH-vil)	A case to protect a private right or to solve a dispute between two people. (Also known as common law)	Un caso para la protección de un derecho privado o para resolver una disputa entre dos personas. (También conocida como ley común)
Common law (KAH-mun)	Law based on court decisions rather than written law; originally, ordinary, everyday laws of England that were not written down.	Leyes basadas en decisiones de las cortes en vez de en las leyes ya escritas. Originalmente, leyes comunes y diarias en Inglaterra que no se fueron puestas por escrito.
Compensation (kom-pen-SAY-shun)	Payment for an injury.	Pagos recibidos por daños y perjuicios.
Confess (kun-FES)	To admit one's guilt or involvement to an official; this must be done by one's own choice.	Admisión de culpa o de involucramiento a un oficial. Esto debe de ser hecho por decisión propia.
Confidential (kon-fih-DEN-shul)	Private, sometimes secret information.	Unformación privada, a veces secreta.
Constitution (kon-stih-TOO-shun)	The basic law that governs the United States, or the paper on which that law is described.	La ley básica de que gobierna los Estados Unidos. El papel donde se describe esta ley.
Contempt of court (kun-TEMPT)	A refusal to obey the order of the court or a show of disrespect for the court and its authority.	El rehusar obediencia a las órdenes de la corte o mostrar falta de respeto por la corte y su autoridad.
Convict (kun-VIKT)	To decide that a person is guilty of a crime and must be sentenced.	Cuando se ha decidido que una persona es culpable de haber cometido un delito y debe ser sentenciada.
Convicted (kun-VIK-ted)	To have been found guilty of a crime in court, usually by a jury.	Haber sido hallado culpable de un delito en corte, usualmente por un jurado.

GLOSSARY

Corrections (kuh-REK-shuns)	Punishment that tries to improve prisoners and make them understand how they have hurt society.	Castigo que trata de mejorar a los prisioneros y hacerles entender como han hecho daño a la sociedad.
Counterfeit (COWN-tur-fit)	An imitation of something, usually money, made to cheat people; a fake copy.	Una imitación de algo, usualmente dinero, hecho para hacerle trampas a la gente. Una copia falsa.
Crime (krym)	An action or act that breaks the law.	Una acción o acto que rompe la ley.
Criminal (KRIH-mih-nul)	A case in which a person is accused of intent to commit or actually committing a serious crime.	Un caso en el cual una persona es acusada de intencionalmente cometer o tratar de cometer un delito serio.
Criminal record (KRIH-mih-nul REH-kurd)	A list of crimes that a person has been accused or convicted of; usually kept by a government agency.	Una lista de delitos que una persona ha sido acusada de cometer o por los cuales ha sido sentenciado. Usualmente los guarda una agencia del gobierno.
Cross examine (kraws ek-ZAH-min)	To question a witness who is testifying for the other side.	La interrogación de un testigo que esta testificando para el lado contrario.
Custody (KUS-tuh-dee)	Being kept by the police or other authorities.	Estar detenido por la policía u otras autoridades
Date rape	Forcible sexual relations with a date.	Relaciones sexuales forzadas durante una salida social.
Death penalty (deth PEH-nul-tee)	When the punishment for a crime is the taking of the convicted person's life; also called capital punishment.	Cuando el castigo para un delito es quitar la vida al sentenciado. También se le llama pena capital.
Defend (dee-FEHND)	To answer the charges against a person.	Responder a los cargos contra una persona.
Double jeopardy (DUH-bul JEH-per-dee)	To be tried for a crime a second time once you have been acquitted, or cleared, of the crime.	Ser juzgado por un delito por segunda vez después de haber sido declarado inocente o exonerado de ese delito.
Due process (dyoo PRAH-ses)	Protection for someone accused of a crime; these include knowing when a hearing will be held, have a hearing, the right to a lawyer, and the right to a fair trial by an impartial jury.	Protección para alguien acusado de un delito. Esto incluye saber cuando una audiencia sera celebrada, el derecho a un abogado y el derecho a un juicio justo por un jurado imparcial.
Elderly abuse (EHL-dur-lee uh-BYOOS)	Mistreatment, in any form, of older people.	Maltrato, en cualquier forma, a una persona mayor.
Embezzlement (em-BEH-zul-ment)	Taking property that someone has trusted you with.	Quedarse con una propiedad que alguien le ha confiado.
Enforce (en-FORS)	To carry out the law effectively.	Hacer cumplir la ley con efectividad.
Evidence (EH-vih-dents)	Proof legally given at a trial; it can be testimony from witnesses, papers, pictures, or any object that has to do with the crime.	Prueba legalmente dada en un juicio. Esta puede ser testimonio de testigos, papeles, fotografías o cualquier objeto que tenga que ver con el delito.
Expert witness (EK-spurt WIT-nes)	Someone who has special knowledge, skill, or experience in the subject of his or her testimony; for example, and expert in guns.	Alguien que tiene un conocimiento especial o experiencia en el topico de su testimonio, por ejemplo, un experto en armas de fuego.

GLOSSARY

Extortion (eks-TAWR-shun)	Threatening someone to get money or property.	El amenazar a alguien para obtener dinero o propiedad.
Federal (FEH-duh-rul)	Having to do with all of the United States.	Relacionado con todos los Estados Unidos.
Felony (FEH-luh-nee)	A major or serious crime; for example, receiving stolen property valued at more that $100 is a felony; punishment for committing a felony is usually more than a year in prison.	Un delito mayor o serio, por ejemplo, recibir propiedad robada valorada por mas de $100 es una felonía. El castigo por cometer una felonía es usualmente mas de un año en la cárcel.
File charges	To accuse someone officially of committing a crime.	Acusar a alguien oficialmente de cometer un delito.
Fine	A sum of money that a guilty person must pay as part of punishment.	Una suma de dinero que una persona culpable debe pagar como parte de su castigo.
Forgery (FAWR-jeh-ree)	Writing or changing a writing on a document in order to cheat someone of property.	Escribir o cambiar la escritura en un documento para hacer trampas con una propiedad.
Foster care (FAW-stur)	Care from someone other that the family.	Cuidado proveído por personas sin relación familiar.
Frisk (Frisk)	To search by running one's hand over a person's clothing.	Registro efectuado cuando se pasa una mano sobre la ropa de una persona.
Grand jury (JOO-ree)	From twelve to twenty-three people who meet in secret to decide whether or not to bring a person to trial.	De doce a ventitrés personas que se reúnen en secreto para decidir si una persona se trae a juicio o no.
Guilty (GIL-tee)	When a jury finds that the accused did commit a crime.	Cuando un jurado encuentra que el acusado cometió un delito.
Habeas corpus (HAY-bee-us CAWR-poos)	Literally, "you have the body;"a legal paper that brings an accused person into court immediately to make sure that the person is being held legally and he or she is charged with a crime.	Literalmente, "usted tiene el cuerpo". Un documento legal que trae a un acusado a un tribunal inmediatamente para asegurarse que la persona esta siendo detenida legalmente y que esta acusada de un delito.
Harrass (huh-RAS)	To annoy, frighten, or threaten another person, often many times or repeatedly.	Molestar, amedrentar o amenazar a otra persona, a menudo, muchas veces o repetidamente.
Hearing (HEE-reeng)	The time when evidence is heard by an official so that a decision can be made on the basis of the evidence.	El momento cuando un oficial escucha la evidencia para asi llegar a una decisión basada en la evidencia.
Homicide (HAH-mih-syd)	Taking a person's life.	Quitarle la vida a una persona.
Hung jury (JOO-ree)	A jury that cannot unanimously decide the guilt or innocence of the accused.	Un jurado que no puede decidir unánimemente la culpabilidad o inocencia del acusado.
Immigration (im-mih-GRAY-shun)	Coming into a country legally to live and work.	Venir a un país legalmente para vivir y trabajar.
Impartial (im-PAR-shul)	Fair; taking no side; having the opinion before seeing and hearing the evidence.	Justo, sin favoritismos, con una opinion antes de ver y escuchar la evidencia.

GLOSSARY

Incest (IN-sest)	Sexual relationship with a member of the family.	Relación sexual con un miembro de la familia.
Indict (in-DYT)	To accuse formally or officially.	Acusar formalmente u oficialmente.
Injunction (in-JUNK-shun)	A court order to stop a particular activity, such as harassment.	Una órden de la corte para hacer cesar una actividad en particular, tal como el acoso.
Intent (in-TENT)	Understanding by a person for the purpose for, or reason why he or she does, an action.	Entendimiento personal del propósito o la razón por la cual una persona hace algo.
Investigate (in-VEH-stih-gayt)	To find out the details of a crime or a case.	Buscar los detalles de un delito o un caso.
Jail (jayl)	A place where people are kept either while they wait for trial or sentencing or while they serve a sentence for a misdemeanor.	Un lugar donde se mantiene a las personas mientras esperan por juicio o sentencia o mientras cumplen un sentencia por un delito menor.
Jeopardy	The danger of being convicted or punished.	El estar en peligro de ser sentenciado o castigado.
Judge (juhj)	To decide upon in court.	Decidir en una corte.
Jury (JOO-ree)	A group of responsible people from the community who must give a verdict on a legal matter.	Un grupo de personas responsables en la comunidad quienes deben dar un veredicto en una cuestión legal.
Larceny (LAR-seh-nee)	Stealing or taking something that does not belong to you.	Robar o tomar algo que no le pertenece.
Line up (LYN-uhp)	A group of people that includes a suspect so that witnesses can try to pick out the suspect.	Un grupo de personas que incluye un sospechoso para que los testigos puedan tratar de identificarlo a este.
Mandatory sentencing (MAN-duh-toh-ree sen-ten-seeng)	A person's sentence for committing a first crime is not long or harsh; if the person is convicted again, the sentence must be longer, no matter how small the crime.	La sentencia dada a una persona al cometer el primer delito no es dura o estricta, si la persona es sentenciada de nuevo esta sentencia debe ser mas larga sin importar cuan pequeño es el delito.
Manslaughter (MAN-slaw-ter)	Taking a person's life without planning it or because the killer acted in a dangerous way.	Quitarle la vida a una persona sin haberlo planeado o porque el asesino actuó en forma peligrosa.
Martial art (MAR-shul)	One of several defense and combat techniques that are usually practiced as sports.	Una de varias técnicas de defensa y combate que son usualmente practicadas como deporte.
Mediation (mee-dee-AY-shun)	A Method of settling an argument outside of court; a third party acts as a link between the arguing people.	Un método de arreglar una disputa fuera de la corte. Cuando una tercera persona actúa como enlace entre las personas en discordia.
Miranda warning (mih-RAN-dah WAR-neeng)	This states that a person must be told of the right to remain silent, that anything he or she says may be used as evidence against him or her, and of the right to have a lawyer present before any questions are asked.	Indica que a una persona se le debe informar que tine el derecho de quedarse callada, que cualquier cosa que diga puede se usado como evidencia en su contra y del derecho de tener a un abogado presente antes de que se le hagan preguntas.

The People's Publishing Group, Inc.: *Crime and the Law*

GLOSSARY

Misdemeanor (mis-deh-MEE-ner)	A minor or less-serious crime; for example, receiving stolen property valued at less that $100 is a misdemeanor; punishment for a misdemeanor is usually less than a year in jail.	Un delito menor o menos serio, for ejemplo, el recibir propiedad robada valorada a menos de $100 es considerado un delito menor y es generalmente menos de un año en la cárcel.
Mistrial (MIS-tryl)	A trial that is ended and declared void (it does not count) because of a few possible reasons, including a hung jury; a new trial could result, or the district attorney might decide to drop the charges.	Un juicio que ha terminado y se ha declarado nulo (que no cuenta) debido a unas cuantas razones posibles, incluyendo un jurado que no ha llegado a una decisión unánime, así puede resultar en un nuevo juicio, o el fiscal puede decidir retirar las acusaciones.
Neglect (nuh-GLEKT)	Not taking proper care of someone in your care; this could be a child, and elderly person, or even a spouse.	No cuidar apropiadamente a alguien bajo su cuidado, puede ser un niño, una persona mayor o un cónyugue.
Negligence (NEH-glih-jints)	Carelessness that causes danger or harm to others.	Descuido que causa peligro o daño otros.
Oath (ohth)	A person's promise in court to tell the truth, the whole truth, and nothing but the truth.	La promesa de una una persona en la corte de decir la verdad, toda la verdad y nada mas que la verdad.
Offense (ah-FENTS)	A crime that can be punished by the law of the state or city where it happened.	Un delito que puede ser castigado por la ley del estado o ciudad donde sucedió.
Organized crime (AWR-gah-nyzd)	A crime that is run like a business.	Delitos que se manejan como un negocio.
Parole (puh-ROHL)	A release that lets a person serve the rest of a sentence outside prison if she or he follows the rules connected with the release.	Un permiso que autoriza a una persona a cumplir el resto de una sentencia fuera de la prisión si esta obedece las reglas conectadas con este permiso.
Patrol (puh-TROHL)	To go through an area on foot or in a car to make sure it is safe and to keep it that way.	Andar por un área a pié o en auto para asegurarse que es segura y para mantenerla así.
Perjury (PUR-joo-ree)	A lie that is told by person who is under oath.	Una mentira dicha por una persona bajo juramento.
Petit jury (puh-TEE JOO-ree)	For six to twelve people who listen to the evidence and decide whether the defendant is guilty or innocent.	Un jurado de seis a doce personas que escuchan la evidencia y deciden si el acusado es culpable o inocente.
Plea (plee)	A statement that you are either guilty or innocent to the charges against you.	Una declaración de que usted es culpable o inocente de los cargos en su contra.
Plea bargaining (plee BAR-gah-neeng)	The accused and the prosecutor negotiate an end to the case; the defendant may give evidence in the case; the defendant may give evidence in the case to help the district attorney or may plead guilty to a lesser offense or to only some of the charges; in return, the defendant asks for a shorter sentence or a reduction of the charges against him.	El acusado y el fiscal negocian un final al caso. El acusado puede dar evidencia en el caso para ayudar a la fiscalía o puede declararse culpable a una ofensa menor o a sólo algunos de los cargos, por esto, el acusado pide una sentencia mas corta o una reducción de los cargos en su contra.
Police force (poh-LEES)	All the police officers in an are; they are usually broken down into groups called police squads.	Todos los oficiales de la policía en un área. Usualmente se dividen en grupos llamados unidades de patrullaje.

Police report (poh-LEES REE-pawrt)	A legal record of the crime; written proof that it was told to the police.	Un informe legal del delito. Una prueba escrita de lo que fué dicho a la policía.
Poverty (PAH-vur-tee)	A situation in which people lack the basic needs--food, money, clothing, and shelter--to live; this situation is usually aggravated by a lack of employment and other social problems.	Una situación en la cual les falta a las personas sus necesidades básicas—comida, dinero, ropa y techo—para vivir, esta situación usualmente se intensifica por la falta de trabajo y otros problemas sociales.
Preliminary hearing (pree-LIH-mih-neh-ree HEE-reeng)	A court hearing at which the judge must decide whether the district attorney has a good case.	Una audiencia en la cual el juez debe decidir si la fiscalía tiene un buen caso.
Prison (PRIH-zin)	A place where people who are serving long sentences for having committed felonies are kept.	Un lugar donde se mantiene a personas que estan cumpliendo sentencias largas por haber cometido felonías.
Privilege (PRIH-vih-lej)	Private information.	Información privada.
Probable cause (PRAH-bah-bul cawz)	Good reason to believe either that property should be searched or that a person should be searched or arrested.	Una buena razón para creer que una propiedad o persona deben ser registrados o alguien debe ser arrestado.
Probation (proh-BAY-shun)	A defendant found guilty of a crime is released by the court without imprisonment; the defendant is subject to conditions set by the court, usually under the supervision of a court officer.	Un acusado que ha sido hallado culpable de un delito y ha sido dejado en libertad por la corte. Este acusado esta sujeto a condiciones impuestas por la corte, usualmente bajo la supervisión de un oficial.
Prosecute (PRAH-suh-kyoot)	To carry out a case against an accused person.	Llevar un caso en contra de un acusado.
Protection services (proh-TEK-shun SUR-vih-sez)	Government program to help abused people find safety from the abuser.	Un programa del gobierno para ayudar aquellas personas a quien se le ha abusado a encontrar seguridad lejos del que las ha abusado.
Protest (PROH-test)	An organized, public way of showing that you don't approve of something or that you object to something.	Una manera pública y organizada de mostrar que usted no esta de acuerdo con algo o que tiene objeciones.
Public defender (PUH-blik dee-FEN-dur)	A lawyer hired by the government to defend persons who are accused of crimes and who are unable to afford a lawyer.	Un abogado pagado por el gobierno para defender personas que son acusadas de delitos pero no tienen con que pagar un abogado.
Rape	To force another person to have sex; when the other person is under age, it is called statutory rape.	Forzar a otra personas a un acto sexual. Cuando la otra persona es menor de edad se le llama abuso de menores.
Reasonable doubt (REE-zin-ah-bul dowt)	When a juror is less that 100 percent certain about the guilt of an accused person.	Cuando un jurado no esta 100 % seguro acerca de la culpabilidad de un acusado.
Represent (reh-pree-ZENT)	To act for; to speak for.	Actuar y hablar por otra persona.
Responsible (ree-SPAHN-sih-bul)	Able to make decisions and can be depended on to understand what is happening.	El poder hacer decisiones y ser considerado capaz de entenderlo que sucede.
Restitution (reh-stih-TOO-shun)	The act of making good for, or payment of the equal value of, a loss, damage or injury.	El cumplir con el pago de igual valor por una pérdida, daño o lastimadura.

GLOSSARY

Reverse a verdict (ree-VERS; VUR-dikt)	To change to the opposite the decision of a lower court.	Cambiar la decisión de una corte menor.
Routine (roo-TEEN)	An action that is always the same; such as getting up or eating every day at the same time.	Una acción que es siempre la misma.
Search (surch)	To look for evidence.	El buscar evidencia.
Search warrant (surch WAH-runt)	A court order giving police legal authority, or power, to make a search.	Una órden de la corte que le da a la policía autoridad o poder legal para conducir un registro.
Seizure (SEE-zhyoor)	The taking of evidence.	El tomar la evidencia.
Sentence (SEN-tents)	To be punished by order of a court after having been found guilty of committing a crime.	El ser castigado por órden de la corte después de haber sido hallado culpable.
Sexual abuse (SEKS-yoo-ul uh-BYOOS)	This occurs when someone uses another person for sexual reasons; it is usually an adult who uses a child this way, but not always.	Esto ocurre cuando una persona utiliza a otra con propósitos sexuales. Usualmente un adulto puede utilizar a un menor de esta forma, pero no siempre.
Sexual assault (SEKS-yoo-ul uh-SAWLT)	An attack of a sexual nature, committed without the consent of the victim; the victim can be a man, a woman, or a child.	Un ataque de naturaleza sexual cometido sin el consentimiento de la víctima, la cual puede ser un hombre, una mujer o un niño.
Sexual harassment (SEKS-yoo-ul huh RAS-ment)	Behavior toward another person in the form of unwanted sexual looks, touches, gestures, or words.	Comportamiento hacia otra persona en forma de miradas, contactos, gestos o palabras sexuales no deseadas.
Skip bail	If you were released on bail after your arrest and don't appear at your trial, you have skipped bail, the money or property that you gave the court and guarantee becomes property of the court.	Si used fue dejado libre bajo fianza después de si arresto y no compareció al jicio,used ha escapado estando bajo fianza y la propiedad que used dió a la corte como garantía se convierte en propiedad de la corte.
STD	Sexually transmitted diseases; these diseases can only be gotten by having sex with someone else who has them; the most serious and deadly STD is AIDS (acquired immune deficiency syndrome).	Enfermedadas trasmitidas sexualmente. Estas enfermedades solo pueden ser adquiridas por contacto sexual con alguien que las tiene. La mas seria y fatal es el SIDA (síndrome de immuno deficiencia adquirida)
Society (soh-SY-eh-tee)	Groups of people living, working, and playing together in a community, town, state, or country.	Grupos de personas que viven, trabajan y disfrutan juntos en una comunidad, ciudad, estado o país.
Spouse abuse (spows uh-BYOOS)	Mistreating a person you are married to; the meaning has been enlarged to include boyfriends and girlfriends; it is also generally called battering.	Maltrato de la persona con la cual se está casado. El significado ha sido extendido para que incluya a los novios y novias. También se le llama agresión.
Statue (STAH-tyoot)	A law.	Una ley.
Subpoena (sub-PEE-nah)	A notice from the court to appear as a witness.	Un aviso de la corte para que usted comparezca como testigo.
Summons (SUH-munz)	A legal notice to appear in court.	Un aviso legal para que usted comparezca a la corte.

GLOSSARY

Supreme Court (soo-PREEM)	The highest court in the United States; its decisions cannot be changed by other courts and must be followed by all.	La corte mas alta de los Estados Unidos. Sus decisiones no pueden ser cambiadas por otras cortes y tienen que ser cumplidas por todas las cortes.
Suspended sentence (suh-SPEND-ded SEN-tents)	A sentence that is not carried out unless the defendant breaks the rules that the court has set.	Una sentencia que no se cumple a menos que el acusado rompa las reglas establecidas por la corte.
Suspicious (suh-SPIH-shus)	Something that might be connected to a crime.	Algo que puede estar conectado a un delito.
Symptoms (SIMP-timz)	Signs of something, such as illness or disease.	Indicaciones de algo, por ejemplo, de una enfermedad.
Testify (TES-tuh-fy)	To give information in court after swearing to tell the truth.	Dar información en corte después de haber prestado juramento de decir la verdad.
Testimony (TEH-stih-mo-nee)	A statement spoken by a witness, under oath, in court.	Una declaración dada por un testigo, bajo juramento, en la corte.
Unfit (un-FIT)	Not capable, usually because of mental or emotional illness.	Incapaz, usualmente debido a enfermedades mentales o emocionales.
Unlawful (un-LAW-ful)	Against the law; illegal.	En contra de la ley. Ilegal.
Vandalism (VAN-duh-lizm)	Doing damage or harm to another person's property.	Hacer daño a la propiedad de otras personas.
Verdict (Vur-dikt)	The decision of the court.	La decisión de la corte.
Vigilante (vih-jih-LAN-tee)	A person who tries to punish crime by himself or as a member of an illegal volunteer group; such groups work outside the criminal justice system.	Una persona que trata de castigar un delito por su cuenta o como miembro de un grupo voluntario ilegal, estos grupos no están reconocidos por el sistema judicial.
Violation (vy-uh-LAY-shun)	Less serious than a misdemeanor, this type of crime is punished by a fine or other punishment, but not by going to jail or prison; also called an infraction.	Menos serio que un delito menor. Este tipo de delito se castiga con una multa u otro castigo, pero no yendo a cárcel o prisión. Se le puede llamar infracción.
White-collar crime (KAH-lur)	The type of crime that usually takes place in an office; examples are embezzlement, forgery, extortion, and income-tax cheating.	El tipo de delito que usualmente toma lugar en una oficina, por ejemplo, desfalco, falsificación, extorsión y trampas en las declaraciones de impuestos.

The People's Publishing Group, Inc.: *Crime and the Law*

BIBLIOGRAPHY

Anger, Power, Violence, and Drugs: Breaking the Connections, by Paul Kivel. Hazelden Educational Materials, The Hazelden Foundation, Minneapolis, 1993.

Criminal Justice, 4th ed., by James A. Inciardi. Harcourt, Brace Jovanovich College Publishers, New York, 1993.

Conflict resolution materials, by Educators for Social Responsibility, 23 Garden Street, Cambridge, Massachusetts 02138.

Law Enforcement News, published by the John Jay College of Criminal Justice, The City University of New York, 899 Tenth Avenue, New York, New York 10019

School Crime and Violence: Victims' Rights, by James A. Rapp, Frank Carrington, and George Nicholson. National School Safety Center, Pepperdine University Press, Malibu, California, revised 1992.

School Safety, the news journal of the National School Safety Center. Pepperdine University, 24255 Pacific Coast Highway, Malibu, California 90263.

Sexual Harassment and Teens: A Program for Positive Change, by Susan Strauss with Pamela Espeland. Free Spirit Publishing Inc., 400 First Avenue North, Suite 616, Minneapolis, Minnesota 55401,

Deadly Consequences: How Violence is Destroying Our Teenage Population and a Plan to Begin Solving the Problem, by Deborah Prothrow-Stith, M.D., with Michaele Weissman. New York, HarperCollins, 1991.

Street Law: A Course in Practical Law, 3rd ed., by Edward T. McMahon, Lee P. Arbetman, and Edward L. O'Brien. National Institute for Citizen Education in the Law, St. Paul, Minnesota, West Publishing Co., 1986.

"*The Fourth R,*" Newsletter of the National Association for Mediation in Education, 425 Amity St., Amherst, Massachusetts 01002.

The Rights of Crime Victims, by James Stark and Howard W. Goldstein, An American Civil Liberties Union Handbook. New York, Bantam Books, 1985.

The Rights of Students, by Janet R. Price, Alan L. Levine, and Eve Cary, An American Civil Liberties Union Handbook. Carbondale and Edwardsville, Illinois, Southern Illinois University Press, 1988.

The Rights of Young People, by Martin Guggenheim and Alan Sussman, An American Civil Liberties Union Handbook. New York, Bantam Books, 1985.

Think About Drugs and Society: Responding to an Epidemic, by Richard A. Hawley. New York, Walker and Company, 1988.

Think About Prisons and the Criminal Justice System, by Lois Smith Owens and Vivian Verdell Gordon. New York, Walker and Company, 1992.

Violence Prevention Curriculum for Adolescents, by Deborah Prothrow-Stith, M.D. Education Development Center, Inc., 55 Chapel St., Newton, Massachusetts 02160.

Juvenile Justice

American Restitution Association (ARA), c/o 232 Horton Hall, Shippensburg University, Shippensburg, Pennsylvania 17257, (803) 744-3381. Persons interested juvenile restitution as victim compensation and accountability. Legal advice and training.

Corrections

Fortune Society, 39 W. 19th Street, 7th Floor, New York, New York 10011, (212) 206-7070. Former offenders and others help former offenders and high-risk youth. Promotes awareness of inmate problems. Helps them secure jobs, literacy training, and counseling. Referrals to half way houses.

Friends Outside, 2105 Hamilton Avenue Suite 290, San Jose, California 95125-5900, (408) 985-8807. Community groups help inmates reenter into society. Sponsors adult, juvenile offender, and victim programs. Obtains emergency services.

Legal Counsel

National Legal Aid and Defender Association (NLADA), 1625 K Street, NW, 8th Floor, Washington, D.C. 20006, (202) 452-0620. Helps organizations giving legal services to the poor in civil or criminal cases. Clearinghouse for legal aid and defender services to the poor. Sponsors research and training.

Witnesses and Victims

WETIP, Inc., PO Box 1296, Rancho Cucamonga, California 91729-1296, (714) 987-5005. Citizens' self-help program to wipe out drug traffic. Helps in arrest of felons. Sponsors the Eyewitness Anonymous Program. Toll-free hotlines are: (800 78-CRIME, (800) 47-ARSON, and (800) 87-FRAUD.

National Organization for Victim Assistance (NOVA), 17577 Park Road, NW, Washington, D.C. 20010, (202) 232-6682. Former victims, legal and health professionals ensure that victims' rights are honored. Counseling, training, and educational. Sponsors National Victim Rights Week.

National Association of Crime Victim Compensation Boards (NACVB), 1601 Connecticut Avenue, NW, Room 201, Washington, D.C. 20004, (202) 332-9070. Creates crime victim compensation programs. Educates the public. Networks with victims' groups. Supports fair legislation for crime victims.

National Association for Crime Victims' Rights (NACVR), PO Box 16161, Portland, Oregon 97216-0161, (503) 252-9012. Local businesses and professionals, through Operation Strike Back, provide a better way than living in fear. Conducts research.

Presents citizen awards. Emergency hotline: (800) 85 CRIME.

Family Violence

National Council on Child Abuse and Family Violence (NCCAFV), 1155 Connecticut Avenue, NW, Suite 400, Washington, D.C. 20036, (202) 429-6695. Supports community prevention programs that help victims of abuse and violence. Educates about family violence. Promotes treatment programs. Toll-free number is (800) 222-2000.

Community Policing

National Association of Town Watch, (NATW), PO Box 303, 7 Wynnewood Road, Suite 215, Wynnewood, Pennsylvania 19096, (215) 649-7055. Watch organizations encourage community crime prevention. Helps with fund raising, promotional materials, and training. Sponsors annual National Night Out, when 7500 communities highlight crime prevention. Gives an award to the best program. Toll-free number: (800) NITE-OUT.

Crime Prevention

Educational Fund to End Handgun Violence (EFEHV), Box 72, 110 Maryland Avenue, NE, Washington, DC 20002, (202) 544-7227. Educates the public about handgun violence education, especially as it affects children. Develops materials and educational programs to convince teens not to carry guns.

American Council for Drug Education, 204 Monroe Street, Suite 110, Rockville, MD 20850, (301)294-0600. Provides information about drug use.